Roz found herself studying his face, his profile.

His hair wasn't all black, she discovered, but was more a deep brown with errant gold highlights here and there. Was that natural? She thought so, and felt the same about the perfectly arched brows above those gorgeous hazel eyes, now hidden by lids sporting ridiculously long eyelashes that curled at the ends. His nose, thin and aquiline, was perfectly proportioned. For the first time, she noticed the merest hint of a mustache and a tiny mole just above and to the right side of pinkish-tan tinted lips.

You are one fine brother.

Pierre opened his eyes. Suddenly, unexpected. Roz was busted.

"Why are you looking at me like that?"

"It's what we journalists do, always examining, looking, probing…"

Pierre eased off the wall and took a step toward Roz. Then another. Roz's heartbeat increased as she watched his gaze take in her face, then move lower to her lips as he licked his own.

He stopped in front of her, separated by inches.

"What are you doing?"

"Examining, searching." He leaned forward, brushed his lips across hers. "Probing…"

Dear Reader,

In 2014, there were back-to-back romance conferences in New Orleans—the perfect excuse to spend almost two weeks in one of the world's liveliest cities. Most activities happened in the fun, famous French Quarter. But what I found even more interesting, and disturbing, was the city that lay outside of those seventy-five square blocks.

Five minutes from the state's biggest tourist attraction and I was quickly reminded of 2005's Hurricane Katrina, the fifth deadliest in our country's history. Ten minutes away and blocks looked much as they did days after the storm. The cameras are gone. The world has forgotten. But many natives, like this book's Pierre LeBlanc, cannot forget because they are still recovering from what happened when the levees broke. Trying to repair their lives. Homes. Hearts. That's where love, and heroine Rosalyn, enter the story. Love can rebuild it all.

Have a zuriday.com!

Zuri Day

FRENCH QUARTER Kisses

ZURI DAY

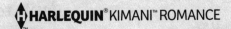

HARLEQUIN® KIMANI™ ROMANCE

Recycling programs
for this product may
not exist in your area.

ISBN-13: 978-1-335-21675-5

French Quarter Kisses

Copyright © 2018 by Zuri Day

For questions and comments about the quality of this book please contact us
at CustomerService@Harlequin.com.

H HARLEQUIN®

™ www.Harlequin.com

Printed in U.S.A.

Zuri Day is the national bestselling author of almost two dozen novels, including the popular Drakes of California series. Her books have earned her a coveted *Publishers Weekly* starred review and a Top Ten Pick out of all the romances featured in *Publishers Weekly* Spring 2014. Day is a winner of the Romance Slam Jam Emma Award and the AALAS (African American Literary Award Show) best romance award, among others, and was a finalist for multiple *RT Book Reviews* Best Book Awards in Multicultural Fiction. Book six in the Drakes of California series, *Crystal Caress*, was voted Book of the Year and garnered her yet another Emma Award in 2016. Her work has been featured in several national publications, including *RT Book Reviews*, *Publishers Weekly*, *Sheen*, *Juicy* and *USA TODAY*. Find out more at zuriday.com.

Books by Zuri Day

Harlequin Kimani Romance

Champagne Kisses
Platinum Promises
Solid Gold Seduction
Secret Silver Nights
Crystal Caress
Silken Embrace
Sapphire Attraction
Lavish Loving
Decadent Desire
French Quarter Kisses

Visit the Author Profile page
at Harlequin.com for more titles.

If you have faced storms and survived.

Came back stronger and better and thrived.

It was life's catalyst, like a lover's first kiss,

That helped you move past fear and fly!

Acknowledgments

A huge thank-you to my fans, the beautiful Daydreamers, who read and support my work. I appreciate you!

Chapter 1

Few knew this, but on August 29, 2005, Hurricane Katrina swept Pierre LeBlanc away from New Orleans on a wave of destruction and despair. Today, more than a decade later, the entire city and, via television sometime later, the entire country, would witness his hometown return amid a flood of bayou-styled fanfare, good wishes and well-deserved praise. It was the Fourth of July weekend, but the festivities felt more like February's Mardi Gras. Drinks steadily flowed. Good times rolled. After experiencing unprecedented success at a Houston-based restaurant called New Orleans, Pierre had finally followed his mentor's advice and opened up his own space. With its innovative take on traditional cuisine, his restaurant, Easy Creole Cuisine, was poised to become the new jewel in the crown of New Orleans's famed French Quarter district. Along with being a new restaurant owner, the onetime shy, almost invisible outcast was now an internationally recognized Chow Channel star and a popular energy drink spokesperson who at the moment was seated on the back of a Rolls-Royce convertible offering slow, easy waves to the throngs of zealous fans welcoming him home.

"Pierre! Over here!"

"Hey, Easy!"

The nickname was one of only a few items that had followed him to Houston. The hometown crowd instantly matched Pierre's laid-back demeanor with the word that appeared on his restaurant's marquee.

"Glad you're back, Easy!"

"Welcome home, Pierre!"

Pierre nodded, waved and offered up his megawatt smile to the fans and photographers shouting his name. Designer shades covered deep hazel eyes, hiding the merest hint of a longtime hurt that never quite went away. Eyes continually surveying, searching, slightly saddened… His sister, Lisette, would meet him at the restaurant. She'd be the only family member on hand to celebrate the big occasion. The other woman who was once in his life, the one that for years he'd searched for online and in the faces of every crowd, had been achingly absent during more than a decade of his life experiences and achieved milestones. His mother, Alana. The woman who'd put her fifteen-year-old son and eleven-year-old daughter on a bus bound for Houston, Texas, promised to meet them there in a week, and disappeared.

The two-car caravan, followed by a small but energetic brass band, reached the restaurant. It was a totally renovated and hugely transformed building originally erected in 1879. The word *Easy* was scrawled across the side and continued upward into the sky in big cursive letters that would light up at night, with the rest of the name, Creole Cuisine, in block letters beneath. That sign and the group of people standing beneath it brought out Pierre's first genuine smile all morning. Hard to believe that the dream he'd held since becoming a line cook and peeling more shrimp than he thought the ocean could hold had finally come true. And that the people who mattered most, well, almost all of them, were here to cheer him on.

Pierre swung a pair of long, lean legs over the side of the car, slid down and waded through a sea of people to hug Lisette, his mentor, Marc Fisher, his second mom, Miss Pat, his network publicist and his newly-hired manager, who'd flown down from New York. Then he walked over to greet the mayor and other city officials standing near the front entrance, just beyond the red ribbon and large bow stretched and waiting to be cut, a symbolic gesture signaling the official opening of Pierre's dream.

"This is a happy day for our city," the mayor said, each word from his booming voice absorbed by the attentive, enamored crowd. "Pierre could have chosen any major city in the country to open his restaurant. We are happy and proud that he has chosen the Big Easy to open Easy Creole Cuisine."

With elaborate fanfare, the mayor was handed a framed proclamation that he read aloud. For the last line, he turned and spoke to Pierre directly. "By the powers vested in me as mayor of New Orleans, I declare this day to be Pierre 'Easy' LeBlanc Day in the city of New Orleans!"

The crowd cheered and began to chant. "Easy! Easy!" And then, "Speech! Speech! Speech!"

Pierre strolled to the microphone and held up his hand to silence the crowd. "Thank you, Mr. Mayor. Thanks to all of the city officials and other public servants who have come out today to lend me your support. I really appreciate it."

Some city officials nodded. Others clapped. The mayor bowed as if to say it was his pleasure as Pierre turned to the crowd.

"And you, the beautiful people of New Orleans! I..." His words were drowned out by the cheering crowd. Pierre waited, then motioned awkwardly for them to calm back down. "This is really incredible. Even though some consider me a celebrity because I'm on the Chow Channel and a product spokesperson for Intensity Energy drinks, I'm still pretty much a regular guy, not much for the spotlight. I usually let my food do the talking, if you know what I'm saying."

Pierre chuckled, a shy, almost self-depreciating sound that came off as especially sexy to the mostly female crowd.

They hung on his every word. Smiled when he smiled. Joined him in laughter. If he were the band leader, they were his orchestra. If he were the quarterback, they were his team. Clearly, he had those around him in the palm of his hand. Several people noticed and weren't surprised. Marc, for instance. His sister, Lisette. Miss Pat. Groupies familiar with his television charisma, who'd helped launch him to superstardom, were even more impressed with his in-person charm. And one woman, a television reporter, seemed prepared to do anything to get the story...and the man.

"I guess the only thing left for me to say is thank you," Pierre finished, his voice soft and sincere. "The next time you're hungry, come on over and get something to eat."

Amid the laughter and applause, Pierre's publicist, Cathy Weiss, a smart, capable young woman working in one of New York's top-notch firms, stepped forward. "We have time for a few questions."

Several reporters asked relevant questions, eliciting sometimes serious, sometimes entertaining answers.

"Eating good food has always been one of my favorite pastimes. But working in a restaurant, New Orleans in Houston, was the first time I considered cooking as a career.

"My inspiration? Definitely my mentor, Marc Fisher, the executive chef at New Orleans. A culinary school and drill sergeant rolled into one. He took me under his wing and encouraged, motivated and threatened my ass into being the best possible chef I could be.

"Other than a chef? I grew up wanting to be an athlete, basketball. And a superhero, when I was five."

The crowd loved listening to Pierre speak from the heart. Clearly, they could have stayed there all day. Just as Cathy walked over to end the questions, a vivacious redhead emerged out of the crowd with microphone in hand.

"Tell me, Pierre," she drawled with an accent that was

part Southern and part seduction. "Is there anything on the menu that is as tasty looking as you?"

"A perfect segue into what's next," Cathy glibly countered, as the crowd reacted, letting Pierre off the hook. "Mayor, if you'll do the honors."

The mayor cut the ribbon. Shortly afterward, eighty lucky diners and eighteen VIP guests sauntered into Easy to put the redhead's unanswered question to the test.

"Oh my God, could she be any more blatant and unprofessional?"

"You act surprised." Rosalyn "Roz" Arnaud didn't look away from her computer screen as she answered Ginny, her coworker at *NO Beat*, a small yet notable New Orleans weekly newspaper.

"Not really. The whole town knows that girl loves men and money."

"That girl" was Roz's former colleague and nemesis, a woman named Brooke who'd worked for years at the city's biggest newspaper. She covered everything from entertainment to sports and considered herself the company's "it" girl. When Roz landed a job there fresh out of college, quickly impressing the higher-ups with her knack for putting an interesting spin on ordinary stories, Brooke had viewed her as competition and tried to make her life there a living hell.

A year into the madness an article Roz had written caught the eye of a guy starting a weekly publication with a focus on local news. He'd offered her a job as senior writer, and the freedom to cover topics she felt passionate about. Roz quit the more established, popular paper, took a salary cut and attached her star to the start-up. A year and a few awards later, *NO Beat* had a small but dedicated staff, national recognition, major advertisers and a solid core of dedicated readers. Turned out Brooke did Roz a favor. Working at *NO Beat* was the best professional decision she could have made.

"Look at him, though," Ginny said dreamily, chin in hand as she gazed at the television. "That bod, those eyes."

Roz gave the screen a cursory glance. Pierre stood at the entrance to his new restaurant, looking the way he had the first time she saw him on an energy drink commercial. Six feet plus of raw sexuality, muscles rippling beneath a tight white shirt as he wrestled a steak off a fiery grill, then reached for a bottle of Intense Energy to refresh him. She remembered being annoyed at how good he looked, and that her body had reacted as though she was a love-starved teen. Truth of the matter was she could use a round of horizontal aerobics, but why tempt fate? It had taken almost a year to get over Delano, her last heartbreak. Today she was in a really good space. She had a job that she loved, covering topics that mattered, a restored twentieth century bungalow, and a terrier named Banner who every day welcomed her home more enthusiastically than any lover ever could. The last thing Roz needed was a pretty boy problem. Especially one that would cause a ten-year journalism vet who knew better to make a comment that bordered on harassment, and reduce sensible women like her coworker Ginny to fantastical would-be nymphs.

"Don't you binge watch him on the Chow Channel?"

Ginny nodded.

"Then why are you acting like you're seeing him for the first time?"

"This is different. He isn't at a television studio in New York. He's here, in our city. Almost close enough for me to touch. Which I would if there was any chance that I could snag a reservation."

"I read where there's a huge waiting list, so good luck with that."

"Yeah, I saw it posted on their website. But there's got to be a way to not have to wait three months for a table."

"Probably, if you have the right connections."

Roz turned back to her computer and the internet research she'd conducted for a month-long series, "Hurricane Katrina Survivors: Where Are They Now?" Solid, serious journalism about a local catastrophe from which even now, more than a dozen years later, the city was still recovering. Amid recent devastating hurricanes like Sandy, Maria and Harvey, Katrina remained the deadliest and costliest one in America's history.

"Do you think Brooke got one?"

"Of course."

"If I know her MO, they'll be dating within the month."

"At least in her mind. Everyone watching TV knows she wants to taste him." Roz delivered the line in Brooke's signature drawl, causing Ginny to break out laughing.

"Can't say I blame her. He could cook for me anytime. And not just in the kitchen. Do you think he has a girlfriend?"

"Who?"

"Mickey Mouse, Roz. Who do you think?"

Again Roz glanced at the mounted TV screen as a handsome, smiling Pierre accepted a key to the city before walking into his restaurant with a sold-out crowd of hungry-looking patrons in tow.

"He's very handsome, I'll give him that. Probably has several girlfriends."

Ginny's look turned wistful as she rested her chin in her palm. "I'd love to be one of them."

"Along with…*her*?"

"Who?"

Both women turned around as their editor-in-chief entered the room. A visionary with a Mohawk haircut and a penchant for tattoos, Andy O'Connor had relocated to the

Big Easy ten years prior, but his East Coast accent wasn't the only reminder of his New York birthplace. He preferred chowder to gumbo, soft rock to cool jazz, and when cut, his blood ran Yankee blue. Everyone adored him.

"Who?" he asked again, reaching for a chip from Roz's bag and munching loudly.

Roz gave him a look. "Help yourself."

"Don't mind if I do." It was said with a wink as he grabbed a handful.

"We're talking about Brooke Evans making an unprofessional public pass at Pierre LeBlanc," Ginny said. "I think he should be a feature next week."

"Should have been this week," Andy replied. "Next week the restaurant opening will be old news."

"True, but he won't."

"Can't argue with that, Gin." Andy swiveled a chair around and straddled it, facing its back. "What would be your angle?"

She shrugged. "The restaurant. His menu. How it feels to be a celebrity chef."

Andy turned to Roz. "What about you?"

"What about me what?"

"What kinds of questions would you ask the city's hometown golden boy?"

"So he's from New Orleans, or just lived here before?"

"Born here," Ginny said confidently. "I checked."

"I'm sure you've Googled him from here to heaven," Andy said to Ginny with a laugh.

"Absolutely. There's a ton of stuff online about his professional life. But very little personal information."

Roz picked up a pen and idly tapped it against the desk. "Since he's from here, I'd ask why he moved to Houston to learn about New Orleans cuisine. And since I'm preparing the series for next month's anniversary, I'd ask him about

Katrina. How it affected him and his family. If that was the reason he moved to Houston. How does the New Orleans he returned to compare to the town he left? There'll be enough stories on his culinary prowess and celebrity stats. My focus would be on the man behind the food."

"That's an excellent angle," Andy said as he rose from the chair. "One I expect you to cover in the first series piece."

Ginny's jaw dropped. Roz's, too.

"Wait! Doing a story on him was my idea."

"It was Ginny's idea," Roz parroted. "She should do the story. She's already done research. Religiously watched his TV show. Aside from him being a chef and spokesperson for the energy drink, I know nothing about the guy and could care even less."

"Which is why you're the perfect one to cover him. No bias. Besides, I've got something else for you, Gin."

"What?" Ginny unashamedly crossed her arms and pouted as though she were two.

"Football."

"The Saints?"

Andy nodded. "Preseason coverage. I've got tickets to the home games, but—"

"Who dat! What? I'm all in."

"I thought you might be. You're the only person I know who likes football more than food."

"Wait a minute. I like football, too." Roz looked at Ginny. "Sure you don't want to switch?"

"Positive," she replied, her voice filled with pure glee. "Pierre's hot, but he's not the breeze."

"So…everybody's happy?" Andy smiled as he eyed Roz's not-so-happy frown on his way out of the room. "Everybody in the country is loving LeBlanc right now," he told her. "Write something great."

Chapter 2

Roz wasn't pleased with her assignment, but after sending inquiries for information and an interview to Pierre's publicist, Cathy Weiss, she spent the next couple weeks on the July articles that had been approved. Crime had increased with the heat index. City Hall was in the middle of another political scandal.

On a lighter note, the whole city united behind eight-year-old child prodigy Zach Johnson, whose keyboard mastery made him America's New Star on the hit TV talent show, with a first prize of a recording contract and half a million dollars. The youngest of seven being raised by a single mother, who'd taken in four more children after her sister died, he and his life-changing win were front page news on *NO Beat* and some national papers, too. Roz met with the entire family for an interview and photo shoot. They were a joy. The kind of people she loved to meet, and the type of story she lived to write.

As August neared Roz switched her focus to the anniversary of Hurricane Katrina and the four-part "Where Are They Now?" series to mark the event. Wanting to start on a high note, she hoped LeBlanc's story would fit the topic, was almost certain she could spin it so that it would. Actually got a little excited about meeting the chef. For business purposes only, she always reminded herself, when at the thought of an "up close and personal" her heart did a little step-ball-chage.

But after spending almost the entire month of July trying to contact him for an interview, she found herself sty-mied. Andy was totally unsympathetic, responding to her woes of the elusive celebrity with "get the story." She scoured the internet for info, then called the restaurant, emailed his publicist, and finally texted a food critic with stellar connections, all several times, to no avail. The restaurant had flat out said he was too busy to be interviewed for at least three months. Cathy had sent a standard press packet and promised to get back to her with answers to the more personalized questions Roz had sent. So far, though? Nothing. The food critic hadn't even bothered to respond. Roz didn't blame him. He was a former associate, an ac-quaintance. Not a friend. Probably thought that she was like every other single woman in New Orleans angling for entry into the chef's private kitchen. Or his bedroom. And not necessarily in that order.

She was frustrated, so after securing the subjects for August's week two and three, and leaving a message for the best friend whose family's story would close out the series, Roz headed over to the other office, where she did her best thinking. Guido's was a bare-bones boxing and workout center that relied on old-school iron rather than modern-day machines to achieve one's desired physique. Roz had discovered it a year ago, when a nasty breakup left her needing something to punch. Hard. Repeatedly. Ginny had suggested the place where her boyfriend sparred thrice weekly with an aggressive punching bag that bobbed and wove but never hit back. Perfect. Roz pounded, weight lifted and squatted out her anger. In the process, she got into the best shape of her life.

"Rozzo!"

"Hey, Gee."

Everyone called the owner of Guido's Gee, pronounced Ghee, short for Guido, even though he was neither vain, uncouth nor Italian. His real name was Gerald, but friends in his high school wrestling circle had dubbed him Guido and the name stuck. Roz surmised that he probably liked "Guido's Gym" better than "Gerald's Gym," anyway.

She stopped at a short counter that served as the modest reception area, where Gee stood frowning at a laptop computer. "What's happening?"

"Trying to figure out this lousy piece of equipment, that's what. That new cook in town heard about my gym and wants to work out here, but his team wanted more info on the place. I'm trying to send it."

"What about your website?"

Gee clicked on it, a basic one-page collection of a few pics, a couple links and not much else.

"You want help?" Roz eased her gym bag off her shoulder and walked around to Gee's side of the counter. He turned the laptop toward her. "Can't believe a pretty boy like him wants to work out in a place like this."

"I think that was supposed to be a compliment so... thanks."

Roz laughed. "It was totally a compliment."

"So you think he's a pretty boy, huh?"

"I think he thinks so. Now, what are we doing here?"

Gee explained what he was trying to send over to the same publicist who'd yet to reply to the questions Roz had sent her. She attached the pictures, included the link to an article ironically written by *NO Beat*, and helped him draft a quick email for the attached. Then she reached for her bag and headed to where three punching bags hung waiting for opponents. Perfect.

An hour later she felt better. Deciding a shower could wait until she got home, she turned to say goodbye to Gee, and walked straight into what felt like a wall.

Actually, it was Pierre LeBlanc.

"Whoa!"

Roz's head snapped around. "I'm sor—*gasp*—Pierre LeBlanc!"

Pierre stepped back, frowning slightly, as two of the guys with him shared a knowing look. *Another adoring fan*, she imagined them thinking. They were no doubt mistaking her breathlessness at having just worked out for infatuation, her wide-eyed surprise as awe instead of shock at literally running into the guy she'd been chasing for almost a month.

"Hi, I'm Rosalyn Arnaud."

"Nice to meet you."

Said without an ounce of sincerity, as after a dismissive glance he brushed past her with what she belatedly recognized as a small entourage. Now hard to miss as she wove through five bodies headed toward the counter. She reached them just as Pierre shook hands with Gee.

A young Hispanic man in the group blocked her path. "He's not interested, okay?"

Roz was not deterred or intimidated. "Neither am I, at least not how you're thinking."

She forced her way past the slight but surprisingly muscular frame and tapped Pierre on the shoulder. "Excuse my intrusion into your personal time, but I've been trying to reach you for weeks. I'm with *NO Beat* and we're doing a series next month to mark the anniversary of Hurricane Katrina. I'd love to lead it off with your story."

"She's one of the best in the business." Gee put an arm around Roz's shoulders. "A straight shooter. Your story is safe with her."

"No, thank you."

"You are from here, right?"

"Yes."

"Were you here for Hurricane Katrina?"

"I'm here now for my restaurant, Easy Creole Cuisine."

Roz watched Pierre scribble his name across the sign-in sheet. Time was running out.

"Do you mind if I ask a few more questions? It'll only take a minute."

"Talk to my publicist. Her contact info is on the website."

"I tried," Roz said to his retreating back.

"Try harder." He threw the words over his shoulder without turning around.

"This will only..." The sentence faded as, seething at the rude way she'd been dismissed, Roz watched his long, sure strides widen the distance between them. "What a jerk."

Gee chuckled.

"Wait, did I say that out loud?"

"Yes, you did."

"Well, he is."

"Ah, don't be so hard on the guy. He probably has women throwing themselves at him 24/7, eight days a week."

"I wasn't one of them," she countered. "My reasons for talking to him were strictly professional."

"If you say so," Gee said. When Roz raised a fist to punch him, he quickly added, "Just playing. I've got to give it to him. Guy's in great shape."

Roz followed Gee's gaze and immediately wished she hadn't. The image would be hard to shake from her mind. Pierre, shirtless. Long black shorts covering a taut butt, hanging off lean hips. Chestnut-colored curls with natural blond highlights that looked so soft Roz's fingers itched to touch them. He chatted with the Hispanic bodyguard who'd tried to block her, while effortlessly lifting a huge barbell up and over his head. His back muscles rippled beneath smooth caramel skin; his arm muscles bulged, then relaxed with each lift and flex. The bodyguard looked over, caught her staring and said something to Pierre, who glanced up. He smiled broadly, then broke out laughing.

Oh, I'm a joke now? "Do you see that, Gee? Is he actually laughing at me?"

The gym owner shook his head. "No, two seconds and you'll see who has his attention."

Just then a tall, busty woman who looked all of a size two breezed by her and headed straight toward Pierre. It was Roz's cue. She turned to Gee. "I'm out."

Roz headed toward the door, totally undeterred. She'd get the story. But now she'd have to go digging for what he could have easily provided. Search out classmates from the middle school he'd attended, the name of which was one of the few nuggets from his past that she'd gleaned online. Better yet, she had a couple contacts who'd grown up in the Ninth Ward, the area hardest hit by Hurricane Katrina and where many who ended up in Houston had lived. Perhaps one of them had known Pierre.

Plan in place, Roz headed toward the door, ready to put in a couple more hours before calling it a day. On the way out she passed a mirror, saw her reflection and did a double take. Sweaty curls bunched in a hasty ponytail. Mascara smudged beneath one eye. Torn T and oversize gray sweats. Unkempt would be a kind description of her appearance. Next to the beautiful woman who'd passed her, Roz looked more like a homeless beggar than a journalist. That still didn't excuse his rudeness. Even the homeless deserved kindness and respect.

Halfway to the car, she heard her phone beep. Roz tapped the message indicator.

Don't forget the ball! I know you're excited. :) Biff

Roz mumbled an expletive as she opened the car door and slid inside. She was so not excited about the Bayou Ball, which was probably why she'd totally forgotten that it was next week. Why had she agreed to attend this prestigious gala and represent both *NO Beat* and her best friend Stefanie's nonprofit organization, Shelter From The Storm? She'd rather get dropped in a war zone and report from the front line. But a promise was a promise. So instead of heading east toward the lower Ninth Ward, Roz whipped around and headed toward the nearest shopping mall.

"Hello, Easy. I'm Rachel. I own Crescent Moon, the bar around the corner from your restaurant."

"It's a pleasure to meet you." He accepted the handshake she offered. "The name's Pierre."

"I thought it was Easy?"

"That, too, I guess."

"It fits you to a T." She stepped closer. "You are definitely easy on the eyes."

Inwardly, Pierre cringed at the unimaginative line and purposely avoided her flirting. "Describes the restaurant's decor even better. A very relaxing atmosphere."

"So I've heard. Looks like it will be a couple months before I can find out for myself, though. Can't believe you're that booked up."

"Me either. It's crazy."

Rachel took a step closer, her barely covered breast brushing Pierre's upper arm. "Are you sure there isn't a way I can…try it out any sooner? Like, as soon as possible?"

Pierre didn't think Rachel was talking about food. He deftly shifted away from the touch as he took in the large breasts spilling over a tight tank top, wondering how she could be so top-heavy and still manage to walk.

"There's a waiting list on our website if you'd like to add your name. So far there have been no cancellations, but it could happen."

"What about a late-night snack after hours? You could join me in the private room at my bar. Drinks on me."

"That's a generous offer, but I can't accept. After putting in eighteen-hour days six or seven days a week, the only place I want to go after locking up is home. And since this is my first day off in almost a month, I'd better get back to this workout."

"Sure thing, gorgeous. Just remember, you always have a free drink waiting at Crescent Moon. Not that you couldn't afford to buy one. Just showing you some neighborly love."

It soon became clear that neighborly love wasn't the only thing Rachel wanted to show. After smiling at Pierre, she walked over to the horizontal crunch bench and lay down. The thong-like leotard she wore left little to the imagination.

Pierre focused on his friends. He deposited the weight back into its holder and strolled over to where his sous chef, Riviera, was doing push-ups on a mat. He dropped down beside him, determined to shake off the constant self-imposed pressure of making his business a success. For him it was not enough to have a great restaurant; Easy Creole Cuisine had to be the best restaurant of its type anywhere. Period. Ensuring that, while juggling other contractual commitments, had sent him to the gym. Misery loves company, so he'd brought along some of the staff, including his out-of-shape manager, Ed, who looked clearly out of place as he held up a wall.

"Come on, Ed!" Pierre aligned his body with Riviera's and matched his quick rhythm. "I want every member on the Easy team to be in shape."

"Yes, Chef, but one day at a time, okay?" Ed palmed both hand weights he'd been pumping, then used a towel to mop up the sweat that ran down his face. "The last time I saw a gym was in high school."

"Remember the prize," Riviera panted, still doing push-ups, but more slowly.

"An all-expense-paid trip to Vegas," Pierre reminded them.

Ed ambled across the floor. "If I keep my knees down, am I a punk?"

"Folks might laugh at you," Riviera warned.

"Let them." Pierre moved next to Ed and placed his own knees on the floor. "When you're fit and healthy, you'll have the last laugh. Twenty-five. Let's go. No excuses."

They finished working out. Pierre endured the guys' ribbing when Rachel insisted on giving him her card before he left the gym. He could appreciate a confident, assertive woman, one who knew what she wanted and went after it. Rachel seemed up for a good time, which right now was all he could give a woman. Unlike the disheveled one who'd claimed to be a reporter, Rachel sent a message that was abundantly clear.

Pierre's current schedule left little room for anything happening in a bed besides sleep. But in a month or so, when the Chow Channel tapings ended and he was confident the kitchen could run smoothly without him, then he'd see.

Chapter 3

An hour before the Bayou Ball was set to begin Roz was no closer to being ready than she'd been two hours ago. She loved red and black, except when *red* went with *carpet*, *black* preceded *tie*, or like tonight, the colors were part of the requested dress code. Heels. Makeup. Social small talk. Who needed that when life was happening all around you?

More importantly, who needed to chance seeing the guy who'd broken your heart barely one year ago? In going to the Bayou Ball being held at the Ritz Carlton hotel, running into her ex, Delano Richard, was inevitable. He never missed a moment to be the center of attention, the city's mover and shaker with all the answers, whose business savvy had made him a multimillionaire. When they first met, Roz was a new edition to the city's number one newspaper. Just beginning her journalism career. Eager to impress. She'd been relentless in her pursuit of the businessman and the story. Transplanted resident promising to restore the famous Ninth Ward, the neighborhood most negatively impacted after Hurricane Katrina. She'd covered him off and on for a year. Developed a friendship that continued past that. And then it went further, to a relationship that Roz thought could go all the way to the altar.

Until she learned that Delano wasn't the man she thought he was, but was using her position and the glowing articles she wrote to enhance his reputation and advance his agenda. He'd counted on love to keep her blinded to his true social-climbing motives until it was too late.

Until he hooked his star to a beautiful socialite, broke up with Roz and broke her heart.

After a six-week whirlwind courtship, the spoiled rich girl had tossed him to the curb. He'd tried to come back to Roz, but that wouldn't happen. Delano had taught her to never, ever mix business with pleasure. And to not trust pretty boys with her heart.

Roz straightened her shoulders. Melancholy morphed into resolve. She'd sworn the last tears over this breakup had been shed long ago. She wasn't going to dredge up more of those emotions. In fact, she was going to cover them up with a sexy dress, some killer heels and a change up from her curly do. Ugly memories of the ex added to frustration at the hard-to-reach celebrity chef she hadn't even wanted to cover. She practically flung the stylish, yet safe, pantsuit she'd planned to wear off her bed and stepped into the walk-in closet. Once there, she released the towel from around her freshly showered bod and reached beyond her normal casual fare for a dress she'd bought on a dare and never worn. It wasn't her style, which, according to the cousin who'd bet money she wouldn't buy it, was the point. Roz pulled it out, turned to the mirror and held the silky, silver maxi with the thigh-high split against herself. She swallowed a lump of shyness, beat back insecurities left over from a childhood of being teased, and took the look even further with a pair of designer stilettos she'd worn only once. The strappy sandals beaded with Swarovski crystals matched the dress perfectly, added just the right amount of bling to the diamond teardrop necklace and matching earrings that she donned for every fancy occasion.

Next she marched into the bathroom and grabbed her curl conqueror from the cabinets below the sink, a gift from the same cousin who'd lost twenty dollars on the dress bet. Roz could count the times she'd used the deluxe flat iron on the fingers of one hand. But she handled the tool and her curls like a pro. Thirty minutes later her hair was straight and long, curled only on the ends, cascading over her shoulders and down her back. When she took a final look in the mirror, all toned and sleek and sexified, she hardly recognized herself. After reaching for her crystal clutch, she flung locks of hair behind her as she headed for the door. Feeling confident and looking the part, she now felt ready to step into society and hold her own against anyone in the room.

Five minutes inside the hotel's ballroom and Roz thanked the gods that she'd changed outfits. All New Orleans's who's who were present. She quickly recognized people she'd grown up with, knew socially or had met in a professional capacity. Unfortunately, one of the first to approach her as she sipped a sparkling water was just about the last person in the room with whom she wanted to converse.

"Hello, Rosalyn."

"Delano."

"You're looking quite beautiful."

"Thank you."

She watched his eyes sweep the area around her. "Rolling solo tonight?"

What's it to you? "Hardly. I know just about everyone in this room."

Delano flashed the dashing smile that used to turn Roz's legs to jelly. Her first victory of the night was that she was truly not moved. "Several of whom would have been happy to be your date. Including me."

"Please."

"What? I'm only stating how I feel."

"Just stop, okay. What we had is long over, never to be revived."

"I messed up, royally. How long are you going to punish me for that?"

"Where is *your* date?"

"I'm looking at her."

"Bye, Delano."

He caught her arm. "Roz, wait."

She pointedly looked down, then up. He immediately released her. "I'm sorry. Listen, can we at least be friends?"

"Let's be friendly, how about that? Cordial while keeping our distance."

"Fair enough." He held out his hand. "To cordiality."

She hesitantly placed her palm in his. Covering her hand with his other one, he looked beyond her and smiled. "Rosalyn, there's someone I want you to meet."

"Maybe later."

He tightened his grip. "He's coming right now."

Roz took a deep breath, bracing herself for a hasty hello and an even faster exit.

"There's the man!" Delano released Roz's hand to greet the person walking up.

"I heard you owned it."

Roz recognized the voice and barely suppressed a groan. The same one that had dismissed her a few days ago, though tonight the tone was friendly, laid-back. She took a deep, calming breath and turned. Good thing, too. Roz wouldn't have thought it possible for the toned, ripped body she saw in the gym to look even better in a tux. But Pierre did.

"Not since you came to town," Delano responded. "Baby…" Roz cut him a look. "I mean, Rosalyn, have you had the pleasure of meeting the city's newest superstar?"

Roz held her poise and a neutral expression as she answered. "We've met."

"I don't think so," Pierre said, an admiring gaze sweeping her from head to toe and back. "There's no way I'd forget meeting someone as lovely as you." He held out his hand. "Pierre LeBlanc."

She placed her hand in his, watched as he lifted it toward his mouth. "Roz Arnaud."

The slightest hesitation before kissing her hand told Roz that he remembered. The evening had just gotten more interesting.

"Rosalyn is a very talented journalist. She works for a newspaper called the *New Orleans Beat*, *NO Beat* for short. It's a smaller, independent publication, but several of their articles have been picked up by the Associated Press, Rosalyn's among them."

"Impressive," Pierre said.

Roz thought so, too. If Delano had paid half as much attention to her while they were dating as he'd obviously done lately, their romance may have had a different ending.

"I'll have to, um, go online and…check out some of your work."

"Have you been to his place?" Delano asked Roz. "Easy Creole Cuisine? Of course you know the name. There's not a person in town who doesn't know who he is."

"Yes, I know about the restaurant, and no, I haven't been there. From what I've heard that's not likely to happen anytime soon."

"You should hook her up, man," Delano said. "Cook a few dishes for her to try out. Get another article for the PR files. There's no such thing as too much publicity."

"I'm sure Pierre is much too busy cooking to speak with a lowly newspaper reporter." Said with a voice of innocence and eyes that feigned understanding.

"No, well, I…"

"Don't worry about it." Roz hated to cut his squirming short, but the one person she wanted to talk with even less than Delano was headed in their direction. "Nice meeting you. Excuse me."

As Roz walked away, Brooke's drawl wafted over the din of noise. "There he is, our hometown hero!"

There she goes, Brooke Evans, the groveler, Roz thought as she continued through the crowd.

Which is why she'll get the interview and the story, said the devil on her shoulder.

If that was the price for keeping her dignity, Roz would pay it. She might regret her actions later, but right now, she just didn't care.

Chapter 4

Newcomers to the Bayou Ball would see a room full of beautiful people, but their eyes would be drawn to a group of distinguished-looking men and one beautiful woman conversing around a highboy table, making an especially impressive tableau. In particular, they'd notice Pierre. The black tux he wore matched close-cropped soft curls and complimented flawless tanned skin. The eyes he normally hid behind shades except when on air or in the kitchen were on full display in all their golden glory.

While the other men hung on every word that Brooke delivered, Pierre subtly scanned the crowd, looking for her. Roz Arnaud, *NO Beat* reporter. Was that really the same women who'd approached him at the gym? Unlikely, he thought, that the woman from Guido's, whose face he could barely remember, was the same beauty who just moments ago had taken his breath away.

"Hey, handsome. Looking for me?"

Pierre felt Brooke's body press up against him. He turned to see that Delano and the other men had left, leaving only him and Brooke at the table. "It's quite a crowd."

"Everyone you need to know is in this room and I know them all. Just say the word and I'll make the proper introductions."

Pierre spotted Roz across the room. "What about her?"

Brooke followed his gaze. "Who, the guy in the white tux?"

"No, the woman he's talking to."

Brooke's smile slipped, but her voice remained chipper. "Roz Arnaud?" She waved a dismissive hand. "Not a part of high society. She tried to be. Snagged a job with my paper right out of college, but couldn't hang in the big leagues. Left and took a job with a small, regional paper, pretty local, actually. Now, the woman behind her is a major socialite whose husband owns—"

"Excuse me. I'm sorry to cut you off," Pierre said as he watched Roz head toward an exit. "But successful people like that don't need me. I'd rather give those small, local businesses my support."

Pierre left a sputtering, confused and chagrined Brooke trying to pick her face up off the floor. He wasn't aware, so mesmerized was he by Roz's natural beauty. She reached the door and was stopped by an older, distinguished-looking couple, which gave Pierre the time he needed to cross the room and catch her arm before she left the room.

"Leaving so soon?"

"And if I am?"

"Then I'm glad that I was able to stop you before you got away." Pierre looked up and saw two women walking toward him with purpose. "Look, can we go somewhere private?"

Without waiting for an answer, he slid his hand from Roz's arm to her hand and gently steered her down the hall to the first opening, a short hallway leading to a set of restrooms. No doubt they wouldn't be alone long.

Roz withdrew her hand from his, but not before Pierre noted her silky, soft skin.

"Okay, Pierre, what is this about?"

"The other day at the gym. That's where we met."

"That's right."

"Wow. You look…totally different."

"I clean up alright."

"More than alright. You're beautiful. I can't believe who I saw the other day is really you."

"Are you saying at the gym you thought I was butt ugly?"

"No!" This wasn't going the way Pierre planned. A small bead of perspiration formed on his neck and rolled down his back. "You were… If I'd known that… I mean…"

"Go ahead. Keep digging."

He pushed sweaty hands into his pockets and leaned against the wall. "I wasn't very nice to you."

"You were rude."

"I didn't think you were really a reporter."

"What then, a troll?"

"No!"

Roz held the frown for a second longer before a chuckle escaped her lips. Pierre exhaled. "Girl, quit teasing. I haven't felt this nervous since high school."

"You thought I was making up being a reporter as a way to spend time with you?"

"Stranger things have happened. You also look very different tonight from…the other day."

"Well, I wasn't faking it. I'm a reporter, one who has called several times to arrange an interview. Did no one give you the message?"

"They may have, but…"

"I also reached out to your publicist, Cathy Weiss?" He nodded. "Before you suggested it, by the way. She told me you were busy, which considering that you're opening a restaurant, I understand. But good publicity never hurt a new business, so I thought at the very least you'd find time to answer the list of questions I sent over."

"I don't remember getting any questions, but that doesn't mean they weren't sent. My emails are overflowing and voice mail stays full. If you really need to reach me Don is your best bet. He's my personal manager and the only one who can reach me 24/7. I can give you his contact info."

"I guess I can send him the questions I sent Cathy, since a personal interview is out of the question."

"Why do you want me so badly? Wait, that came out wrong."

"Ha-ha. It sure did. To be clear, the editor and another writer are the ones who feel you're too relevant not to cover. I can think of half a dozen subjects more worthy of the space."

"Damn, beautiful, why don't you tell me how you really feel?"

"I just did." She smiled, drawing Pierre's eyes to her lips. Lips that were full and moist and ready to be kissed, making him wonder if that fiery personality transferred to the bedroom, and how that looked up close. An errant tendril fell across Roz's eyebrow. Instinctively, he reached up and gently placed it behind her ear. Their eyes met. Was that a flash of desire he saw in the chocolate orbs watching him intently?

She broke the connection, reached into a jeweled clutch and pulled out her cell. "Don...what's his last name?"

"Sanders."

Roz's thumbs flew across the keys. "Number?"

"You haven't been to the restaurant, right?"

"No, I haven't."

"Tell you what. We're closed today, but why don't I make an exception for you and have you come by around... eight or nine, and I'll make a few dishes?"

"Why?"

"How are you going to write about my restaurant if you haven't tasted the food?"

"The food is what everyone is writing about. That's the

obvious angle. I want our focus to be on the man behind the menu."

"So let me get this straight. You're turning down a private dinner at the hottest restaurant in New Orleans?"

"I guess so."

"Come on, now. I'm trying to redeem myself."

"That's admirable, but you know what they say."

"No, what do they say, whoever 'they' are?"

"That you never get a second chance to make a first impression."

"Then will you give me the chance to make an excellent second impression?"

"While conducting an interview?"

"Yes."

"Then, yes, I'll give you that chance. And I have the perfect place to meet. It's not well-known or highbrow, but they make the best local cuisine anywhere."

"You mean besides mine."

"I mean better than anyone, anywhere. Period."

"You want to bet on that?"

"I'd have no problem taking your money if you want to go that route."

"Watch yourself now. Remember, you haven't tried my food. Not a good idea to place a bet that you're guaranteed to lose."

"I'm confident enough to call you on it."

"Okay. What are the stakes?"

He watched Roz ponder the question. "If I win, dinner for my parents at your restaurant. Next week. On the house."

"Done. And if I win?"

"You won't."

"Yes, but just in case I do. What can I have?"

A devilish glint showed in Roz's eye just before she answered with a question of her own. "What do you want?" And then, as if words had rushed out before she could catch them, much as had happened to him earlier when his thoughts of her beauty were voiced out loud, she rushed on. "Wait. Don't answer that. The question came out totally wrong."

"Ha! Too late to back out now." He watched her catch and nibble a portion of her lovely lower lip. "Nervous?"

"No."

She warmed him like sunshine. Pierre wanted more of her heat. He pulled out his phone. "What's the name of this place?"

"It's called Ma's. I don't have the address, but I can text it to you."

They exchanged numbers. A group of women rounded the corner, headed toward the ladies' room. Once they saw Pierre he knew privacy was over. "I look forward to our date," he mumbled as they neared them.

"It's not a date." Roz began walking away. Pierre's touch was tender as he grabbed her arm. She turned around.

"Call it whatever you want to call it, but just remember that when it comes to all things culinary...I usually win."

Chapter 5

"How stupid are you?"

That's what Roz's BFF Stefanie asked when told that Roz had turned down Pierre's invitation for a private dinner after hours in the most sought-after space in town. Roz understood. Stefanie didn't. She hadn't met Pierre up close and personal, felt the animal magnetism that kept Roz tossing and turning all night after the ball, and thinking about him for the rest of the weekend. If Stefanie knew all that, then she'd know that meeting Pierre on neutral territory with people around would keep Roz from doing something she'd later regret.

She arrived early and waited in her car, determined to not make a repeat of their past interactions. Placing bets and blurting out leading questions in a direction she totally intended not to go. It wasn't like her to flip out over a handsome guy. She was neither a starstruck fan nor a bumbling idiot with no command of the English language. She was a serious journalist who knew the price that could be paid for turning a business opportunity into potential pleasure. Embarrassment. Heartbreak. Delano had taught her that.

That the two men knew each other was yet another reason to keep things strictly professional between her and the chef. No telling what her ex had told Pierre about them. Knowing Delano, he wouldn't have kept quiet about their past relationship or been hesitant to throw her under the bus with why it ended.

Roz thought these things and ignored the flutter in her stomach when an image of how Pierre had looked that night swam before her eyes. Ignored how she'd thought of him all day and anticipated this meeting. Told herself she'd gotten there early because she wanted to be there when Pierre arrived, lest he take one look at the humble abode that served as a public eatery and keep on driving.

On one matter, however, she allowed herself to face the truth. When it came to Louisiana cooking, nobody could outdo Manette Lafeyette, whom everyone called Ma. Roz's bestie, Stefanie, had dragged her there the day Roz decided to leave the city's biggest newspaper for the job at *NO Beat*. While she'd been excited about the possibilities attached to the start-up, feeling she'd been forced from the job she'd snagged right after college had left her down in the dumps. That day Roz had learned that anything going wrong in life could be cured with Ma's gumbo. And her crawfish? Lord have mercy. Roz couldn't wait to see Pierre's face when he entered Ma's and was assailed by the aromas that wrapped themselves around you as soon as you walked through the door. Smells that effortlessly pulled you farther into the room. Just thinking of the bucket of crawfish and buttered bread loaf served free with every meal made her mouth water.

Roz got out of her car and checked her watch, anxious now to assuage her grumbling stomach. It had been months since she'd eaten at Ma's. She'd purposely skipped lunch today to enjoy the meal. She checked her watch again, frowned as she looked up…and into Pierre's eyes.

"Am I late?" He'd lowered his window to ask the question before pulling to the curb and parking. He turned off the engine and hopped out of his car.

Those eyes. That smile again. Damn, he was gorgeous. *Don't be affected*, she warned her body. *Don't let it matter*, she told her head.

"Right on time, actually. Hope you're hungry."

"If the food inside looks as good as you do…"

"Don't be average," Roz said, as she rolled her eyes and began walking up the sidewalk toward the house. "Save that for your groupies," she added over her shoulder.

"Groupies? I don't have groupies. And that wasn't a line. You look very nice."

"Then perhaps that's what you should have said."

A smile softened the caustic words as Roz waited until Pierre caught up with her before she opened the small home's screen door and the thick wooden one behind it. She wanted to see the look on his face that she'd seen on so many other Ma first-timers.

"Ready?"

His glance was skeptical. "I guess."

Her smile widened. She opened the inner door. A cacophony of odors rose up like instruments in an orchestra. Oregano harmonizing with garlic and onion. Thyme keeping time with dry mustard and dill seed. Cayenne, smoked paprika and bay leaves adding oomph to the melody. Pierre took two steps. Stopped, closed his eyes and inhaled. Roz laughed.

He opened eyes filled with wonder. "Whose place is this?"

"Mine, and y'all need to get on in here and close the door. I'm not trying to cool off the whole neighborhood."

A petite woman with long white hair and an ageless face that could have been sixty or ninety-six walked toward them. Mouth frowning, eyes beaming.

She reached up to give Roz a hug, all the while looking at the man standing beside her. "Took long enough for you to get back here. Where have you been?"

"Way too long, I know. I've been really busy lately, but I'm so glad I'm here. Just thinking about your food makes my mouth water."

"Hmm." Ma looked at Pierre. "Who is this handsome

young man you've brought to my house?" Her eyes slid back over to Roz. "Is he why you've been busy?"

"What? Oh, no, Ma. This isn't... We're not..."

"Pierre LeBlanc, ma'am." Pierre leaned down to hug Ma, then raised her soft and slightly wrinkled hand to his lips and kissed it. "It smells like I just walked into crayfish heaven, and a whole lot more."

Ma stepped back to look up at him. "What would you know about it? You look way too fancy to know about mudbugs."

"I know a little something about them. Grew up in New Orleans."

"He's a chef, Ma," Roz explained. "Just opened a restaurant in the Quarters, called Easy Creole Cuisine."

"So you think you can cook, huh?" Ma asked.

"I do alright."

"If I ever get to taste something you fix, I'll be the judge of that."

Roz raised her hand to cover a chuckle. Pierre's eyes gleamed as he smiled. "Alright, then."

He took a couple steps and looked around him. "Never would have guessed all of what was going on in this little house." He tipped his head. "Behind that door we just entered."

"That's the way I like it," Ma said, giving him a little shove as she pointed to one of four tables, all unoccupied, in what had originally been a living room. "Don't want the city coming in here bothering me, telling me what to use and how to use it."

"How do you get your customers?"

"How'd you come here?"

"Word of mouth." He nodded, looking paradoxically comfortable as he sat in a plastic chair that might have been around at least half as long as Ma. "Well, if the food tastes half as good as it smells..."

"It tastes even better." Roz took a chair to his right, facing the door. She placed her purse on one of two empty chairs at their table and pulled out a small recorder. "Do you mind?"

"What's that for?"

"With the smells assaulting your senses I can understand you forgetting what brought us here. Our interview."

"Oh, right. That." He shrugged. "I guess I don't mind. Depends on what you ask me."

"Fair enough. If you want to share something off the record just let me know."

"Does that really work?"

"What?"

"Sharing something off the record." He used air quotes to underscore his distrust.

"Depends on the reporter. There is a code of ethics that most professional journalists follow. I'm a member of the Society of Professional Journalists, the organization that established the code in 1909."

"Then how do magazines get away with printing any and everything about celebrities and people they don't even know?"

"Clearly, everyone who writes and prints a story does not follow that code. But don't worry. Given you're already the city's golden boy, I'd imagine this chat will be pretty painless."

"Y'all go wash your hands!" The command yelled from the kitchen caused a raised brow.

"You don't want to disobey her," Roz whispered, scooting back her chair to comply. When the two returned, Ma had set two lemon waters on a table now covered with newspaper. She came up behind them swinging a small bucket in one hand, holding a small loaf of buttered French bread in the other.

"Bone appetite," she said, purposely mispronouncing

the famous French phrase as she set down the fare, along with two large "napkins," otherwise called hand towels.

Pierre leaned into the steam rising from the bucket and inhaled. "Wow." He positioned the towel over his lap and prepared to dig in.

Roz made a sound that stopped him. "Um, ladies first?"

"Ladies better hurry."

"Ha!" Roz reached into the bucket and pulled out what was alternately called a crawfish, crawdad, crayfish or baby lobster, depending on who you asked. She felt Pierre's eyes on her as, with a quick twist of the wrist, she separated the body from the crawfish head. With unabashed pleasure she placed the latter in her mouth and sucked out the juicy meatiness inside. After tossing the shell on the newspaper, she made quick work of slurping the remaining meat from the tail while reaching for her next one.

"Obviously not your first bucket," Pierre quipped as he picked up one of the Louisiana delicacies and devoured it the same as Roz.

"Nope."

"You from here?"

"Born and bred. Only recently developed a love for crawfish, though. My mom hates them and refused their presence in our home."

"Where'd you grow up?"

"Eastover."

"Ah, one of those."

Roz frowned as she shamelessly licked juice from her fingers. "What do you mean by that?"

"Girls from your part of town had nothing to do with us boys in the Ninth Ward."

"Is that where you grew up?"

"Spent a lot of time there" was Pierre's vague answer.

"Well, I can't speak for the girls you met back then, but I was not a part of the popular girl crowd."

Pierre eyed her as he twisted the head from another crawfish. "I find that hard to believe."

"Well, believe it. I was tall, skinny, with a head too big for the slender neck beneath it. I was too light in some places and too dark in others. In other words, I often didn't fit in anywhere."

Pierre's eyes narrowed seductively. "Clearly all of that's changed. You are…lovely."

"When I look in the mirror I still see the socially awkward bookworm."

"Everyone else sees someone beautiful, educated, successful. Someone with the world in the palm of her hand."

"I guess you'd know."

"Me?"

"Of course. Superstar chef with the world as your oyster, probably with a trail of broken hearts scattered down Interstate 10."

"Not even close. What you see of my life now looks nothing like it did growing up."

"In this area?"

"Sometimes."

"Where else?"

"Didn't matter where. The results were the same."

"According to what I've read, being here mattered in 2005. You were here when Katrina hit."

"Until the water pushed us out and I landed in Houston."

"Tell me about that. It's the angle for my story. New Orleanians who experienced Katrina to survive and thrive."

Pierre nodded, slowly and thoughtfully. "What would you like to know?"

Roz wiped her hands on the towel and reached for her water. "Everything."

Chapter 6

So easy to talk to, Pierre thought, as he considered her question. He, too, wiped his hands and sat back in the hard plastic chair. When he did his eyes dropped to the recorder. Sure, she was beautiful, and dismantled one of his favorite crustaceans like a pro, but she was a reporter. Of course talking to her would be easy. Maybe too easy. She'd been taught how to coax information from individuals, make them feel comfortable. Catch them off guard. If this was what her schooling, training and experience had taught her, Pierre thought, she must have graduated at the top of her class. She was very good at her job.

So good that Pierre had almost forgotten some very important rules. He didn't talk about his past, especially Katrina. Because to talk about Katrina, he'd have to talk about family. To talk about family, he'd have to talk about his mom, and Grand-Mère Juliette. Pull the scab off the wound left by his grandmother's and mom's disappearance during the storm. He still called it that, a disappearance, even though with all the time passed he was sure that they'd met the same fate as thousands of others whose lives had ended in a watery grave. The mom whose last words had been *"Take care of your sister. I'll see y'all soon. Promise."*

Only she hadn't arrived in Houston. She'd broken her promise. Which was why to this day there wasn't a woman he could trust.

Especially one who'd set a recorder between them. He

shifted in his seat, saw Ma carrying a heavily laden tray out of the kitchen, and was thankful for her timing.

"Here, let me help you with that."

"I've carried heavier burdens in my lifetime," Ma insisted, though she readily allowed Pierre to take the tray of steamy goodness and place it on the table beside them, while Roz, knowing the drill, carefully bunched up the newspaper and placed it in the now empty red bucket.

"What all do we have here?" Pierre removed two small bowls from the tray, lifting one to his nostrils before setting it down. "Red beans and rice with, what's that, andouille or boudin?"

"Neither. That's Ma's sausage. None else like it nowhere."

He stepped back so Ma could set down piping-hot plates of jambalaya being transferred from the tray to the table.

"Ma, this all looks amazing," Roz said.

"Smells even better than it looks," Pierre added.

Ma replied in her traditional fashion. "Bone appetite."

He'd barely sat down before picking up his fork to spear a chunk of sausage swimming in the bowl of beans and rice. He placed the nugget in his mouth and closed his eyes as he began to chew.

"The usual suspects," he began, still chewing. "Thyme, paprika, bay leaf, sage…" Swallowing, he turned admiring eyes toward Ma. "But what's that sweet undertone? Nutmeg? Ginger?"

"That's for me to know and for you to never find out. Knowing that here is the only place you can get it will keep you coming back."

"No doubt, I'll be back." Pierre tested the jambalaya. "Ma, this is divine. I need to spend some time in your kitchen."

"I guess I could use a dishwasher from time to time." She winked at Roz while Pierre laughed, and walked back into the kitchen, a smile clearly showing that his compliments were appreciated.

For the next few minutes, the deliciousness of Ma's food dominated the conversation. But midway through the jambalaya, Roz repeated her earlier question to Pierre.

"You were telling me about your experience during Hurricane Katrina. What was that like?"

"You first. Where were you when it hit?"

"Out of state, Columbia, Missouri, preparing to enter my first year at Mizzou." At Pierre's raised brows she added, "University of Missouri."

"Why didn't you attend college here?"

"I wanted to. My mom wanted me to go to Southern, or Tulane. But my dad is a Midwesterner and felt that spending time outside my home state would broaden my cultural horizons. Plus, the University of Missouri has one of the best journalism programs in the country. So it wasn't a long argument. Dad won.

"Watching that storm on TV, and the events that unfolded afterward, was surreal. I couldn't wrap my mind around the videos I saw and the town I knew. I wanted to come back and cover it, write an article for the school paper. Of course, my parents forbade it. Too dangerous. I was livid, sure I could cover the events in a way foreigners couldn't. Foreigners being anyone not from New Orleans.

"Looking back, I know they were right. I may have been ready to write a story, but I wouldn't have been ready to see in person the aftermath we all witnessed on TV, or handle the emotional and psychological aftereffects."

Having dealt with those aftereffects for more than a decade, Pierre understood.

Both became quiet—somber, reflective, remembering a moment in history that few who witnessed it could ever forget. Pierre wanted to, wished he could, and continued to steer the focus away from those painful memories.

"They made it out, your family?"

"Yes," Roz answered. "Our home wasn't in the major flood area, but my parents didn't want to take any chances. One of my uncles lives in Atlanta. They left before the storm hit. What about you? Where were you when it happened?"

"A few blocks over."

"From where we are now?"

He nodded.

"In one of the areas hardest hit. That had to have been a painfully frightening experience."

"It was."

"Did you have to be rescued?"

"Almost. We were able to get on one of the buses headed to Houston where…we have family."

"So your whole family was displaced. Mom, dad…"

"My sister and I."

"And your parents stayed here?"

"My mother raised us. She stayed behind to help my grandmother. It was a traumatizing experience that's hard to talk about. I survived it by focusing on what was ahead of me, not by looking back."

"Yet while living in Houston you ended up at a restaurant called New Orleans."

"It wasn't planned."

"How did it happen, you working at a restaurant that bears your hometown's name?"

Pierre shrugged. "Needed money."

"McDonald's wasn't hiring?"

"I'll admit that the name of the place drew me in. I missed the food we're known for and wondered if the place lived up to it name. Of course, I couldn't afford to order a meal. So I asked for a job instead."

"Ingenuity in action."

"More like desperation, but whatever, it worked."

"They hired you as…"

Pierre smiled and looked toward the kitchen. "A dishwasher. And to my great surprise the food was delicious, just like back home. I was there for about a month, glad to be eating good and earning a steady paycheck, when one of the prep cooks quit unexpectedly and I volunteered to take over. The work was tedious, but the kitchen atmosphere— infectious. The workers loved and often fought like family. But during service all hostilities were dropped for the sake of synchronicity. That's when I discovered the mechanical and scientific aspects of cooking, the work that went into each perfect plate. Marc orchestrated each player's movements like a conductor leading an orchestra. Everyone's role was important, from dishwasher to head chef. Don't get me wrong. The work is hard, the hours long. And if you're running the kitchen, it can consume your life. But I found it fascinating, began staying late and coming in early, learning how the kitchen ran, how things got done. Marc noticed my interest and took me under his wing. My culinary journey continued from there."

"Your ability to adapt is impressive, especially after such a horrific experience. And you were how old? Nineteen, twenty?"

Pierre looked sheepish as he answered, "Fifteen."

"Didn't that go against child labor laws?"

"It may have, had they known it. But I could easily pass for seventeen at that point and that is what I put on the application."

"Did your boss ever find out?"

"When he took me in and I had to change high schools, I also had to come clean about my real age."

"So you went to live with your mentor? Why?"

"Wasn't working out where I was."

"With your mom and sister?"

"Things always remained cool with my sister. It was me and the rest of the household that didn't see eye to eye. Marc saw I was troubled and wanted to know why. When I told him, he offered me his spare bedroom. Taking him up on that offer was the best decision I could have made. Undoubtedly changed my life."

"Katrina, though devastating, led you to your destiny."

"I guess so."

"So you believe you survived because the restaurant gave you focus."

"Focus. Family. Goals. Motivation. Marc was like a father figure to me. Still is."

"Did you know your father?"

Pierre shook his head.

"Did your family situation ever smooth out in Houston?"

After a long pause, he nodded. "Yes."

"Does your mom still live there?"

"No."

He hadn't meant for the word to come out so harshly, but he didn't want to discuss his mother.

"Where do you think you'd be had Katrina not happened and you'd stayed here in New Orleans?"

"That's a good question," he replied. One that Pierre had never asked himself. When the answer floated into his mind it surprised him, but he looked at Roz and answered truthfully. "Probably dead."

Instinctively, she reached over and placed her hand on his forearm. "The streets can be dangerous. I'm glad you escaped them."

"Me, too. I plan to pay it forward by doing for others here what Marc did for me in Houston. By teaching some of this city's young men the joy of cooking, a lesson that teaches many other skills, as well."

"What are you going to call it?"

"I don't know yet. The idea is just a dream right now. I have my hands full getting this new business up and running."

"Well, whenever it happens, the program sounds wonderful. Tell me more about it."

Pierre did, becoming more talkative and animated as he expounded on his passion for cooking and for mentoring young men. Aside from Marc and Lisette, he hadn't mentioned his dream to anyone, not even his sous chef, Riviera, who he planned to recruit to be a part of his mentoring team. It also helped that talking about the program took them away from speaking about floods and family.

They talked for two hours, leaving only when Ma threatened to make them help her clean up. Once outside, the two became quiet. Surprising, but Pierre knew what was on his mind. He wanted more conversations with this probing reporter, ones when she was not on the clock. Did she feel the same way?

"So, Mr. LeBlanc, was that as painful as you thought it would be?"

"Not at all. For a supposedly socially awkward sister, you're not so bad."

Roz gave him a look. "You're not what I expected either."

"What did you expect?"

"Someone more shallow and self-absorbed. I mean, you may very well possess those traits, but I thank you that tonight at least you've kept them to yourself."

"Ha!"

Roz held out her hand. "Seriously, it was a good interview. When it's up online, I'll send you a link."

"You can do me one better," Pierre replied, returning

Roz's handshake and once again noticing her soft skin. "You can bring a copy over to the restaurant and then stay for lunch or dinner, whichever works, on the house."

"I thought you were sold out."

"We are. But I'm the boss. I can make exceptions."

"Thank you, but…I'm not sure that's a good idea."

"What, eating?"

"Accepting your invitation for a free meal. There may be strings attached."

"Will you feel better paying for it? Seems rather disingenuous to write about a restaurant you've not even visited."

"I thought that was settled. The article will be about you, not the food. But put that way, I guess it would be advantageous to come to your establishment and find out what all the hype is about, a visit that could lead to a follow-up story."

"What about Wednesday evening, around nine?"

"This Wednesday?"

"Yes."

"Isn't nine o'clock rather late?"

"Yes, but the kitchen isn't as slammed at that hour. I could put all my focus on tantalizing your taste buds."

Pierre watched Roz nibble the side of her lip as she thought. "Okay, Wednesday at Easy Creole Cuisine."

"Cool. See you then."

She reached her car, opened the door and then turned around. "Oh, and Pierre?"

"Yes."

"I won, so thanks for my parent's reservation, as well."

Roz's smile was mischievous, smug even. Pierre started toward her but she slid behind the wheel, started the car and sped away. Clearly, she wanted to have the last word.

Pulling away from the curb, he played back those last few minutes. The devilish glint in Roz's eye as she boldly proclaimed victory regarding the bet. How her brow scrunched each time she nibbled her lip. How before saying yes to his invitation she'd darted her tongue out to moisten those tempting, cushy lips. He wondered how soft they were, and how long he'd have to wait to find out. A kiss was definitely in their future. That and much more. Roz may have won the food bet but after tonight Pierre was clear about the next thing he wanted to win. Her.

Chapter 7

There was more to Pierre's story. Roz saw it in his eyes, could feel it in her gut. What he'd shared was interesting and would make a great piece. She had a feeling that what he didn't say would make an even better one. Avoiding questions about his mom. Reluctance to talk about his family at all. Vague answers when asked about his early life in New Orleans… Those gorgeous green-flecked copper eyes tinged with a type of sadness that made her want to wipe it away. That fleeting look of vulnerability that, dammit, slipped past the armor around her heart and touched her soul. That made her want to tell him everything was going to turn out fine. Hadn't that happened already?

It was as though she could still see that teenager inside him. The one uprooted by a storm, forced to navigate a new city and move in with a stranger. What had happened in his home life to cause that drastic action? Roz realized she'd ended the evening with more questions than answers. She wanted the rest of the story, had an opportunity to get it on Wednesday night. Dinner at Easy Creole Cuisine. He said there were no strings, but was there more to that, too? Another question popped up as Roz stopped for a red light. Did she want there to be?

Her phone rang. As the light turned green and she eased through the intersection, Roz tapped the car's Bluetooth.

"Hey, Biff!"

"What's happening, Biff?"

It's what Roz and childhood pal Stefanie Powell had

called each other since their preteen years, after hearing the term "BFF" in an episode of *Friends*. They'd added an *i* to be unique.

"Same old, same old. Are you in town?"

"Just touched down and headed to baggage claim as we speak. Want to come get me?"

"I'd love to, but I'm on deadline."

"Aren't you always on deadline?"

"Pretty much."

"Working on the anniversary articles?"

"Absolutely, and guess what. I just finished an interview with Pierre LeBlanc."

"After turning down his invitation for a private dinner? I'm surprised he invited you back."

"He didn't. We ate at Ma's."

"Quit playing."

"What?"

"Tell me you did not take that man to the hood."

Stefanie sounded so righteously indignant that Roz had to milk the moment.

"Why not? It's my favorite place!"

"Because you can't mix caviar with crawdads, that's why!"

"He calls them crayfish and loves them even more than me."

"So let me get this straight. You interviewed the owner of the city's hottest restaurant where it's almost impossible to get a table not at said establishment but in a matchbox of a house with an old woman serving up gumbo in her living room."

"I wanted him to experience the best Creole cooking anywhere. Ma's is it."

"Only you," she said with a sigh so dramatic Roz could almost feel Stefanie's breath.

Roz guffawed.

"I don't find this funny. You may not have wanted to eat there but you have friends…"

"Oh, I'll eat there. I have a reservation for Wednesday."

Stefanie squealed. "Now there's my smart biff! I wondered where the alien I've been speaking to had taken her. The rez is for me, you and who else?"

"Not so fast," Roz said, laughing. "I didn't exactly secure a table. Pierre invited me as a result of the interview. He didn't say I could bring a guest and I didn't ask."

"But you will now."

"Stefanie, this is work."

"Tell him it's work for me, too. I'll bring my camera."

"Now there's a thought. It would be great to get a few shots to accompany the article."

"Perfect. The magazine might even be interested in doing a spread on him. He's not a model, but he's got a body built for fashion. That Intense Energy commercial is really popular. I'm sure our fitness addict editor-in-chief is a fan. She might even give him the cover."

"Listen to you, living your photography dreams, and with a major magazine. I'm so proud. How's New York?"

"Big. Crowded. Loud. Dirty. Expensive. Hot as hell right now. And I wouldn't want to be anywhere else."

"Ha! Okay, that's more like it."

"I'm so excited about going to Easy Creole Cuisine!"

"Calm down, chickie. You're not confirmed yet!"

"I'm still excited. But let's talk about what's really important. Is he as gorgeous up close as he is on TV?"

"I've only seen the Intense Energy commercials, and no."

"You're kidding."

"He looks even better."

"Ooh, I'm so jealous. So…did you two hit it off?"

"Our meeting wasn't like that. It was an interview."

"I'm not your boss. You don't have to be Miss Professional with me."

"I'm not."

"Roz, I know you. There's no way you were around that guy and didn't feel a flutter somewhere. Your kitty probably started doing Kegels on its own."

A laugh flew out of Roz's mouth. "You're stupid!"

"That means I'm right."

"It means you're stupid and if things don't work out at the magazine, you should try comedy. Maybe amateur night at the Apollo."

"You, on the other hand, should stick to writing stories, not jokes. Now, act like I'm your best friend and share your secrets about the chef."

"Hate to disappoint you but there are none. You know I don't mix work and pleasure. Yes, he's very attractive and yes, I was very attracted, but I'm not interested."

"Why not? Is he married, engaged, gay, off the market?"

"He's off-limits for me."

"Please don't tell me this is about Delano, and you swearing off prospects met during working hours. You're working 90 percent of the time."

"I'm not a workaholic."

"You're not a nun either, but you're acting like one. When is the last time you got some?"

"I can't believe you just asked me that."

"That long, huh? Look, if you're not interested I'll take a shot at him."

"You'll do no such thing. Have you forgotten you're engaged?"

"Almost. That man is fine enough to make me forget my name!"

Roz shook her head, chuckling as she pulled into her

bungalow's detached garage. "I'm home now and getting ready to work. I'll call you later."

"You'd better. I'll need to know the time of our reservations. Okay, bye."

"Bye. Oh wait, Stef—"

All that talk about Pierre, and Roz had forgotten to share her plans to include Stefanie's family in the Katrina series, too, and pay tribute to Aaron, Stefanie's brother who died in the flood. There you had it. That Pierre was a major distraction had just been proved.

Roz entered the house and after taking her Yorkie for a quick walk and talking with her mom, settled in front of her laptop to write Pierre's story. It was a perfect blend of fact and fantasy, stats and story of turning lemons into lemonade, or in the case of an Orleanian, lemon ice. She looked up the New Orleans restaurant in Houston, found Marc Fisher's contact info and sent an email requesting a promotional photo of him, preferably doing his thing in the kitchen, and asking if he happened to have any of Pierre from his early days there. Those juxtaposed with a couple that Stefanie could shoot of him in and around Easy Creole Cuisine would make a perfect journalistic package.

After a few revisions, Roz sent a copy to the proofer and another one to Andy. She sent a text to Pierre requesting a Friday night reservation for her parents and permission to bring a photographer with her on Wednesday. A two-letter reply came back almost immediately: Ok.

Roz forwarded the answer to Stefanie, and while she laughed at the Omgggggggggg that her BFF sent back in response to meeting the man many called Easy, Roz secretly admitted that a part of her was excited to see him, too.

Wednesday came and Roz found herself navigating the Quarter, a part of town where locals rarely ventured. In summer it was always crowded, but as the oversize yet stylish sign reading Easy Creole Cuisine came into view, traffic slowed to a standstill. People were everywhere. Ten minutes and she'd barely moved a car length.

Roz tapped speed dial on the car's Bluetooth. Stefanie picked up before the second ring. "I was just about to dial you."

"Are you here?"

"I'm standing across the street from the restaurant, and it's madness!"

Roz was seeing that firsthand. And she could barely hear. She turned up the volume. "Did you valet?"

"No, and you won't be able to either. I hear that the Drakes showed up, the entire family, and have basically shut the place down!"

"Who are the Drakes?"

"As in Drake Wines?"

"I don't think I've had it."

"Maybe not, but you know them. One of the brothers, Reginald, lives here. He's a co-owner of the New Orleans Brass baseball team! You can't not know the Drakes. The family's a frickin' dynasty."

"If you say so."

"Remember Ace underwear, that fine chocolate drop with the brightly colored boxers?"

"Who doesn't remember those commercials? He's there?"

"Yes, with his wife, London, the model. Maiden name, Drake."

"Oh, I know who you're talking about now. She dated that weird director and then got married to the designer. I never connected that Ace to the underwear ads. No wonder there's a crowd."

"Not just them. It's a family of stars. One sister is a dancer on Broadway. One of the brothers is a big-time politician, a senator or governor or something."

"Niko Drake! The one who faced off with the president and got the health bill amended to where basically no American could be denied treatment for any reason."

"Told you that you knew them. The family has businesses all over California—brothers, cousins, in-laws who together run several successful companies, including a seven-star winery and spa."

"No wonder traffic's backed up. But listen. Stay where you are. A friend of mine manages a hotel two blocks over. I'll park my car there and meet you. Right across the street from Easy Creole Cuisine?"

"Yes, but I don't think we'll be able to get in. There's a guy resembling a boulder at the door and a line of people waiting that I haven't seen move."

"Our invitation is from the owner of the company. We'll be fine."

Roz parked her car and found her friend. It had taken less than fifteen minutes to do so, and in that short time, the crowd had swelled even more. With Stefanie at her heels, she maneuvered around hawkers and gawkers, feeling special as she bypassed the line and walked to the door. A big, bouncer-type dude wearing shades at night blocked it.

"Sorry, ladies. There's no going inside."

"My name is Roz Arnaud with *NO Beat*. We're guests of the chef."

"Everyone in that line feels the same way."

"No, seriously, I interviewed Pierre for our paper and he invited me to the restaurant to try out the food. This is Stefanie Powell, our photographer."

Stefanie held up her digital Canon.

Buddy the Bouncer hooked a thumb the size of a turkey leg behind them. "You see that? The restaurant's full. It's a private event. VIP. I've been given explicit instructions to not let anyone in. You have a problem with that, you're going to have to take it up with the boss."

Roz pulled out her phone and called Pierre. Voice mail. *That's just great.* "Hi, Pierre, it's Roz with *NO Beat*. We're here at the restaurant doors but can't get in."

"Blocked by the Rock of Gibraltar," Stefanie mumbled, in spite of Roz's nudge.

"If you get this in the next few minutes, please let your guard here know that we've been invited. Thanks."

She ended the call, dropped the phone into her purse and put a couple feet between her and King Kong.

He followed them. "Ladies, you can't stand here. You'll have to go back down the stairs."

It felt like the walk of shame as they turned around and walked down the steps they'd confidently pranced up just seconds before. And even though it meant walking three extra blocks, they turned right instead of left to avoid the smirks of those they'd sashayed by who were standing in line.

"I am so embarrassed," Roz hissed, as she pulled out her phone and sent a text.

"I'm just hungry," Stefanie replied. "And my feet hurt. These are my walk-a-block-and-sit-my-ass-down pair of shoes. Not the ones to walk all over the Quarter."

"I'm sorry."

"It's okay."

"Wonder if Ma's is open."

"Let's find out."

Chapter 8

The normally calm, orchestrated chaos of Pierre's kitchen had been interrupted. Usually a party of ten would have been no big deal, even for a sold-out house. The private rooms were not counted in the dining room total, allowing Pierre the flexibility to make last-minute changes. Good thing, since it took both private rooms to accommodate the Drakes. His pleasure, of course. Pierre wore Ace's fashions. The restaurant carried Drake Wines. His personal welcome had led to an invitation to spend a week at their California winery. If he survived the crazy success of his opening and could grab a week, maybe six months from now, he'd be ready for a resort and spa. Heading back into the kitchen, he admitted that his body could use one now.

He'd started off the party with his signature seafood gumbo and platters of Cajun-seasoned lobster lollipops, gator balls and creamed corn beignets. Now they worked on a variety of entrees, including a special request from one who had the audacity to come to a restaurant offering premium seafood and order vegan. It was a challenge, but a good chef could create a meal from air. In the time it took to walk from the private room to the kitchen, he'd mentally concocted a unique dish that he now executed, flipping with one hand and seasoning with the other, while barking orders, checking times and watching the expediter eye every plate before it went out. Everything had to be perfect.

"Time on that tender?"

"Three minutes, Chef!"

"More sauce under those crab cakes, Mell."

"Yes, Chef."

"Riviera, these salmon steaks are perfect. Good job."

"Thank you, Chef."

Two hours later, the Drake entourage made a quiet exit by slipping out the back door to limos waiting in the alley. With the VIPs gone, the dining room finally emptying out and all the signature dishes under control, Pierre turned the kitchen over to his sous chef, went into his office and collapsed on the love seat just inside the door. Seconds later Buddha, one of only two friends who remained from childhood, who had pulled impromptu guard duty at Pierre's urgent request, tapped on the door before stepping inside.

"Here you go, boss."

Pierre reached for the cold bottle of water Buddha offered. "Thanks, man. And thanks for helping out tonight. I don't know what would have happened without you on the door."

"That was crazy, man. I've bounced at a lot of clubs and that scene was crazier than all those times put together. Good thing my man was close and in his squad car."

"So it was you who called the police?"

"A friend of mine on the force, but yes, had to, unless you wanted a riot!"

"People trying to get in, guests not leaving…"

"And that model London…wow! That is one fine woman." Buddha shook his head slowly, licking his lips and rubbing massive paws that passed for hands together as though ready to enjoy a meal.

"She's beautiful, and she knows it."

"Yeah, and I know it, too." Buddha took a long swig of water. "Tell me that if she'd invited you to go with her, you wouldn't have been out of here in a second."

"I would have stayed right in my kitchen with the kinds of flames I know how to handle."

"People were trying everything to get inside. This one chick even claimed to be your special guest. She—"

Pierre sat straight up. "Roz!"

"Who?"

"Oh, no! In all of the hoopla I forgot all about her. Why didn't you let her in?"

"My job was to keep everybody out!"

"But she was my guest."

"I didn't know!"

Pierre pulled out his phone. It vibrated in his hand with texts, missed calls and voice mail. He scrolled through the messages, recognizing Roz's number when he reached it. Unsure whether he really wanted to know what she'd said, he opened the text, anyway.

The next time you invite someone to your restaurant, you might consider letting them in. The link to the article. R.

He sighed and flopped back in the love seat.

"I'm sorry, man. Was that your girl or something?"

"She's a reporter who did a story on me and the restaurant. I invited her here because she'd never tried my cooking." *And to make up for my rude behavior during our first meeting.* "And because she'd had a hard time reaching me or getting info from Cathy."

"And thanks to me she got blocked again."

"You didn't know." Pierre began typing a reply and then, on second thought, clicked on her phone number. "Hey, man, I need a minute."

"Oh, okay. I'm going to head out."

"I'll call you. Thanks again."

After four rings, Pierre expected the call to go to voice mail. He was formulating a message when she answered.

"Roz, it's Pierre."

"I recognized the number."

"I thought you weren't going to pick up."

"I almost didn't."

"About tonight…"

"Didn't go as planned?"

"No, I wasn't expecting a mega superstar to come to my restaurant and have thousands of her fans trying to come in with her. Everything happened at once. It was a madhouse, and in the middle of all that, time got away from me and… I'm sorry."

"It's okay."

"Not really. I invited you to my establishment and should have made sure you were able to get in. I understand if you're upset."

"I was pretty ticked earlier. But considering the circumstances, you had your hands full."

"True, but I feel badly that you and your friend were turned away."

"Me, too. She's a photographer and we were going to do a spread for a second article that would have run sometime in the future."

"What are you doing Monday?"

"Working, why?"

"If you'd like you can hang out with me, get your pictures and a behind-the-scenes look at a day in the life of a chef."

"That's a generous offer, but really, I'm good. One turn with your bodyguard was enough for me."

"I will personally be at the door to let you in. Please, let me make up for the way you were treated."

"I'll check with my boss and let you know."

"Okay. I look forward to seeing you then."

Pierre propped his feet on the desk and clicked on the link in Roz's text. It was a good article. He knew that even though he wasn't much of a reader. He determined that because of how reading the article on him by "Rosalyn Arnaud," according to the byline, made him feel. It was almost as though he was reading about someone else's life. Heck, when he finished what she'd written, his own story inspired him!

The euphoric feeling was short-lived. Pierre knew that as good as what he'd shared with her sounded, it wasn't the whole story. Had he told the rest of it, there would not have been a happy ending. In that moment he felt the weight that came from hiding a large part of himself for over a decade. Re-creating history into a story more palatable to hear, and to tell. Lies by omission. The family relocated to Houston. Was it his fault that most assumed that family included parents, a mom and a dad? And that Miss Pat was a second mom, because the first one had vanished and was probably dead?

"Chef, you got a minute?"

"Sure, Pete. Come on in."

Pierre clicked off the online article and suddenly recalled why he'd left the kitchen in the first place—to double a previous order after learning the estimates he'd calculated for prawns, lobster and crayfish were not enough. Business had crashed into his thoughts in time to stave off melancholy. Fortunately, when you had a hit TV show, repped the number one energy drink in the country and ran the most popular restaurant in the city, you didn't have time to dwell on what was missing from life. What filled his life up these days was pretty amazing. Pierre chose to focus on that.

"We've got a special request from a table of ten, the birthday dinner happening at eight."

"Yes, what is it?"

"Um, it's rather unusual."

"What do they want, a special type of cake that's not on the menu?"

"Basically."

"Okay, what kind?"

"One large enough for you to pop out of after the guest of honor blows out the candles."

"You're kidding, right?"

"Totally serious. The woman who called, a best friend, said you're the birthday guest's favorite everything. She's sure you'll be mentioned somewhere in her birthday wish."

"Maybe, but me jumping out of a cake isn't going to happen."

"They're willing to pay extra."

"Doesn't matter."

"Even if the extra is twenty-five thousand bucks? That's the price she quoted."

"Even for two-hundred and fifty thousand. I'm not on the menu. Period."

"Can I jump out of it, then? Our firstborn will be here any minute and that would buy a lot of diapers."

"Hey, they've booked the private room, so if you can work it out, fine by me."

Pierre checked in with his sous chef and then called it a night. In the early days of his celebrity, there were many casual hookups and meaningless sex romps. No matter how delightful that sounded to the average man, those no-name liaisons satisfied for only so long before the soul wanted connection, the mind sought intellectual intimacy. With this thought came an image of Roz Arnaud. Pierre looked forward to Monday.

Chapter 9

That night, Roz left a message for Andy about covering a day in the life of their celebrity chef, but by Monday morning, as she paired black skinny jeans with a tan top and sandals, and hurriedly brushed errant curls into a high ponytail, she hadn't heard back. So the next step after backing out of her garage and putting the car in Drive was engaging her Bluetooth to call her boss's cell.

"What's up, Roz?"

"Did you get my message?"

"Yes, but I didn't get why. We already ran that story."

"Yes, but an even bigger one happened Saturday night." She told Andy about the Drakes descending on the Big Easy. "Through him we might get an interview with Reginald Drake, co-owner of the—"

"New Orleans Brass. Everybody knows that."

"I didn't. Anyway, a high-profile interview like that would be huge."

"What time is this meeting?"

Roz glanced at her watch. "In about thirty minutes."

"Why so early when the place doesn't open until mid-afternoon? If I were talking to Ginny I'd know the answer. Are you all gaga, too?"

Totally. "Of course not. And because the question came from you, I won't get offended."

Andy chuckled. "Tell you what. I'll give you the day to work in the field if you give me the lead on Reggie."

"Deal."

"Oh, Andy. I need to take this call. I'll check in later." Roz switched lanes as she switched calls. "Morning, Stef."

"Hey, Biff. Sorry I missed your call last night. I wanted to thank you again for honoring Aaron's memory in the anniversary series. Mom is so excited. Dad, too. He'll be at the office, but said feel free to give him a call."

"Good old Deacon Powell. Always ready with a sound bite."

"You know it."

"And I always look forward to spending time with your mom. Unfortunately, Biff, it can't be today. I've got to cover another time-sensitive story. Is there any way I can move you guys to tomorrow?"

"Sure, that's fine. I fly home this afternoon, but the parents will be here and we can talk by phone. What's this news you need to cover? Anything exciting?"

"No, not really. Just heading over to Easy Creole Cuisine to spend some one-on-one time with Pierre LeBlanc."

"What!" Stefanie held the word like a note to a song. "Ooh, Roz. I knew you wanted to take a bite out of that butterscotch bar. I don't blame you, girl. Just let me know how it tastes!"

"LeBlanc may not be on the menu, but I'm pretty excited."

"Y'all talked the other night?"

"Yes. He responded to the sarcastic text I sent after our summary dismissal from the steps of his establishment. He seemed really sorry that we got turned away."

"Then why aren't *we* heading to his place right now?"

"Because this is work, Stefanie."

"Yeah, he'll have to blow through, what, a year's worth of dust?"

"Shut up!" Roz managed to gasp, while cracking up laughing.

"But after the sex, then what?"

"Then I hang up because I'm almost there."

"Call me later."

"Will do."

Pierre had texted Roz to use one of the restaurant's reserved parking spaces across the street. As she pulled in, two images raised immediate concern. Why was King Kong and not Pierre waiting at the front door as promised, and why was there a helicopter on the roof? Roz grabbed her purse and her keys and set out to get her questions answered.

The big guy smiled as she approached. A positive sign.

"Don't worry," he said, raising his hands as if she were the bad guy. "I'm not here to turn you away."

"That's a good thing."

"Sorry about the other night. That was my fault. I'm Buddha."

Roz's brow arched as her hand was engulfed by his as they shook. "Roz Arnaud."

"Trust me, I know who you are."

What did that mean?

He opened the door. She walked inside, but instead of continuing straight into the dining room, he turned toward a hall. "Come this way."

Behind a door at the end of the hall was a set of stairs. Before she could think to ask Buddha where they were going, they reached the roof, where Pierre stood conversing with another man. He immediately came over.

"Good morning, beautiful." He leaned in for a hug, smelling like musk and sunshine, then delivered a smile that could cure cancer. "I see the two of you have met. I wanted you to know that beneath that formidable frame is a big teddy bear."

Roz nodded. "Emphasis on *big*."

"Nice meeting you, Roz." Buddha turned to Pierre with a fist bump. "See you later, Easy."

"Easy is really your nickname?"

"That's what the clique called me back in the day. None of us used our real names. Easygoing Pierre was shortened to Easy. Bernard became Buddha."

"Ah, now I get it." She turned toward the helicopter. "But I don't get that. What is a chopper doing on the roof of your building, and why am I standing next to it?"

"Oh, I didn't tell you?"

"Tell me what?"

"That my life today happens in New York?"

"No, you didn't."

Pierre smiled as he raised a knuckle and brushed her cheek. "Right off the bat, you're getting a taste of my life. Flexibility is key. Change happens often. You've got to be ready for anything." He reached for her hand. "Are you ready for anything?"

Roz swallowed her fear, grasped his hand and gave him an answer. "Yes."

Chapter 10

Thankfully, the helicopter ride was brief, landing at the New Orleans Lakefront Airport. Roz had barely wrapped her mind around the fact that the day wasn't happening at Easy Creole Cuisine, or in New Orleans, before she was being helped out of the helicopter and walking hand in hand with Pierre to a private plane.

While he talked with the pilot, Roz settled into a roomy leather seat. Soon, he sat across from her and buckled up.

"So this is how you celebrities do it? Nice."

"Only when it's on someone else's dime. This is the company behind Intense Energy. I'm shooting some stuff for them today and if we finish early enough I'll drop by the Chow Channel."

"How often do you fly to New York?"

"Fairly often."

"For the Chow Channel mostly?"

"That and a couple other business interests. Plus, I like the city."

"You sound like my friend Stefanie. The one who came with me to the restaurant the other night and was turned away."

Pierre grimaced. "Ouch."

"She said she'd accept a free meal as your apology."

"Done."

The pilot announced they were ready for takeoff. Once airborne, they continued conversing.

"Did you have to try out to get on the Chow Channel?"

Pierre shook his head. "That was a fluke. I'd done some video in the kitchen at New Orleans, preparing a couple dishes, just messing around really. One of their producers came across it on YouTube and called me up and… here I am."

"Lucky break."

"Indeed."

"And the energy drink, Intense Energy?"

"That happened through someone I met in New York who worked with the company. She told me they were looking for a face for their brand. I have a face. So I went to the audition."

Roz smiled. "Had you ever done anything like that before?"

"Never."

"Then how'd you know it was something you wanted?"

"I'd heard how much money the spokesperson would be making."

"Ah, that's a motivator. Did you beat out a lot of people?"

"A couple hundred."

"Wow. Impressive."

"I think my friend may have put in a good word for me. It also helped that I was on the Chow Channel and had a following."

"So you're a Chow Channel star, the face of the number one energy drink and have just opened a restaurant with a backlog of reservations and rave reviews. For someone who had a front row seat to one of the country's most devastating hurricanes, and was basically forced into adulthood at age fifteen, you done good."

"Thanks."

"Your mom must be so proud."

Roz watched the smile on his face dissipate. He nodded, but said not a word. She wisely changed the subject.

Over the next two hours they talked about everything from places they'd traveled to favorite foods. Roz learned that they shared a love for tennis, Thai food and old-school jazz. While not having much to say about his mom, Pierre talked extensively about his mentor at New Orleans, and the life-changing move from urban Houston to Marc's home in the suburbs. The more they talked, the more she felt Pierre relax and begin to open up.

Time flew by, and when they touched down in the Big Apple, the pace increased even more. Roz took copious notes as Pierre breezed through filming at Intense Energy, handling all the attention with ease. He gave each person who stopped him his undivided attention. Fan, cameraman, producer, cabdriver—he treated everyone kindly, and with respect. By the time they arrived at the Chow Channel, Roz knew firsthand just how much work Pierre packed into a day.

After watching him flex for Intense Energy and smile while cooking for the Chow Channel crew, she realized something else. She was pretty sure that she'd fallen in love with him. Yep, gaga, like every other female who had eyes and breathed.

Almost eight hours after arriving in New York, Pierre and Roz said goodbye to the folks at Chow Channel, which marked an end to his day.

"Did you enjoy that?"

"Every minute! It was fantastic!"

"I see the excitement in your eyes."

"No one knows how hard you guys work behind the scenes."

"At the restaurant we have a saying. 'Being easy is hard work.'"

"Ha! That I now know for sure."

They got on the elevator. He became quiet, head back,

eyes closed as he leaned against the cool metal of the wall. Roz found herself studying his face, his profile. His hair wasn't black, but a rich, dark brown with blond highlights some women paid to achieve. His looked natural, as did his perfectly arched brows above those gorgeous eyes now hidden by lids sporting ridiculously long eyelashes that curled at the ends. His nose, thin and aquiline, was perfectly proportioned. For the first time she noticed the merest hint of a mustache and a tiny mole just above and to the right of pinkish, tan-tinted lips.

You are one fine brother.

Pierre opened his eyes, suddenly, unexpectedly. Roz was busted.

"Why are you looking at me like that?"

"It's what we journalists do, always examining, looking, probing…"

Pierre eased off the wall and took a step toward her. Then another. Roz's heartbeat increased as she watched his eyes take in her face, then lower to her lips as he licked his own.

He stopped in front of her, separated by inches.

"What are you doing?"

"Examining, searching." He leaned forward, brushed his lips across hers. "Probing…"

He kissed her again, pressed his groin against her. Roz took a breath, which was all the opening Pierre needed to slip his tongue inside. Examining, searching, probing…

The elevator stopped. Pierre reached up and tweaked a hardened nipple as he stepped back, adjusted himself, letting Roz know that he was hard, too.

"I have a place up in Harlem. Would you like to see it?"

Roz knew what he asked wasn't one question, but several. She had one answer for all of them.

"Yes."

During the thirty-minute ride from the Chow Channel studios in Chelsea to his two-bedroom, two-bath condo just off 110th Avenue, Pierre's behavior was friendly, but platonic. Given the way Roz's body hungered for his touch, the space between them in the spacious Town Car back seat felt as wide as the Hudson, which they traveled alongside. He entertained her with tales of his first time in New York and getting lost on the subway, falling in love with Broadway and Times Square and eating his way through New York's plethora of neighborhoods—from Little Italy and Chinatown in Lower Manhattan to French African and Jamaican fare on Harlem's Striver's Row. Pierre kept his hands to himself as they entered the lobby and rode the elevator to the seventeenth floor. But as soon as they entered his home and closed the door, it was clear that he still had an appetite, and she was the dish he desired.

The assault started at the door, where he pulled her around and placed her against it, sandwiching her with his body, crushing her lips as he pulled at her top. She wanted to stop him or at the very least tell him to slow down, take it easy. But her hands had other ideas, as even while these thoughts played in her mind, she reached for his belt and frantically undid the buckle. They parted just long enough to pull off this, push down that and toss the clothes aside. He picked her up then, his hands gripping bare ample buns that hung on either side of a lacy pink thong as he walked them to the bedroom and lowered her to the bed—gently, almost reverently, as though she was precious and rare. Only then did he pause to stare at her body, the effect evident as she watched him grow harder before her eyes.

"I'm sorry," he said, trying to bring his breathing under control. "It's been a while and you're so beautiful and I just want to…"

He dropped to his knees, bent to her ankles and kissed a trail from there to her thigh, all while searching for and finding her landing spot, its moisture evident as his hand swept her thong. After lavishing the same attention on the other leg, he removed the sandals she still wore and let his boxers hit the ground.

Lord. Have. Mercy.

Roz bit her lip, tried to not to writhe with anticipation of what was to come. Delano, her ex, had treated oral like a gift unwrapped only on special occasions, like a birthday, graduation or anniversary. But here it was her first time with Pierre and already his tongue drew lazy circles on her thigh, then licked a line to her heat. He swiped the slit between her folds, rubbing the lace against her now hard and supersensitive bud. Roz grabbed the spread, her body arching with an almost primal need for direct contact, long and deep.

"Please," she whispered, softly and to herself, hoping that he hadn't heard her.

But he had. He pulled the fabric aside and increased his assault. Burying his tongue inside her as he lapped her nectar and teased her pearl. He raised her legs and spread them, leaving her open and exposed for his thorough tonguing. Roz felt she would die from the pleasure and tried to push away from him. But he gripped her legs and held her firm—swirling, sucking, flicking, kissing her there—until the orgasmic ecstasy that had begun in her toes pulsated through her body and caused an explosion, the likes of which Roz had not known was possible. It took a few seconds before she realized the hoarse scream reaching her ears was her own. Her legs trembled uncontrollably, but before she could try and stop them, indeed before she could hardly move at all, Pierre had sheathed himself and begun a slow, tight descent inside her. He held himself back, gave her body time to adjust. And when it did, he made slow, deep, powerful love to the deepest part of her being. Made love to her soul. Roz had thought him dangerous. Now she knew it. Pierre didn't have a lethal weapon, he was one. She knew something else.

It was time to live dangerously.

Chapter 11

Later, after the two had recovered from the strenuous workout and Pierre had belatedly given Roz a tour of his modern, compact and cozy love lair, he suggested they spend the night in New York, and wake up tomorrow for round two. Tempting, but Roz declined. She needed to write while the notes were fresh, and knew Andy would want to see results from her day in the field. So after a shower, during which she turned on the water and turned off her thoughts, they headed back to the airport for a quiet ride home.

Roz woke up the next morning to sore thighs and mixed emotions. Yesterday had been the best day of her life and the worst that could happen at the same time. Pierre was an excellent lover, easily the best she'd ever had. She'd broken her own rule about not sleeping with subject matter. The thought had come several kisses, forbidden touches and an orgasm too late, and she still felt guilty about it. Stefanie would tell her to stop being so serious. To shrug it off and chalk it up to a night of great sex. But her body wanted more than one night. And so did her heart.

"Turn it off, Roz," she mumbled, easing out of bed and heading for coffee.

But despite what she told herself, she couldn't do it. Everything about him was sexy. After Delano, she should have been immune to Pierre's physical charm. She'd thought she was. Yet some light flirtation, a private flight and a whirlwind afternoon in New York and her will had folded like cheap origami. Folded like hundreds, maybe even thousands before her. *Way to set yourself apart, Roz.*

Sleeping with Pierre was probably the wrong move. So why had it felt so right last night? Didn't matter. It happened. One-night stand. Probably over. Time to move on. After calling Mrs. Powell to confirm their appointment, she sent Andy the article written last night and reminded him of her midmorning appointment that day. Once in the car, she called Stefanie.

"Hey, Roz!"

"Hey, Stef."

"So…"

"Don't get mad at what I'm going to tell you, because everything was out of my hands."

"What, you didn't get the reservation? Girl, please. I don't care about that."

"I flew to New York yesterday."

"Youdidwhat?" Stefanie rushed three words into one.

"So not long after we hung up I arrived at Easy Creole Cuisine."

"Uh-huh."

"And when I got there a helicopter was on the roof."

"Get out."

"No kidding. And King Kong, who I now know as Buddha, was at the door."

"You came here with Pierre?"

"Yes."

"What? And didn't call me? Text…nothing?"

"I know, it's crazy. Everything happened so fast. One place after the other. I barely had time to catch my breath before we were on to the next thing."

"I can't believe you. Start at the beginning. Tell me everything. Don't leave anything out."

"Can't right now. I'm not that far from your parents'

house and my appointment with your mom. I'll call you
tonight and share everything, but I will tell you this."

Roz paused for effect.

"You slept with him."

"I shouldn't have, but oh my God, Stefanie. It was amazing. I'll call you later and tell you about the whole day."

"I can't wait. So are you seeing him again today?"

"I doubt it. I haven't heard from him and I'm not going
to call him."

"Look, turn off that analytical mind and let your heart
lead you. And if not that, your—"

"Bye, Stefanie!"

Her best friend's laughter was loud and contagious. Roz
couldn't help chuckling as she walked to the porch. Even
with the sadness of discussing Stefanie's brother Aaron's
untimely passing, Roz finished the interview and still felt
good the rest of the day.

The week passed quickly. Pierre hadn't called Roz, but
he'd thought about her every day. Not just the sex, which
was amazing. But how good he felt just hanging out. Her
inquisitiveness and zest for life. How she was interested
in everything going on around her. How much he enjoyed
their conversation. How comfortable he felt in her silence.
Was he ready for a relationship? Pierre put the question
on hold and focused on work. But he knew it would have
to be answered sooner rather than later. From everything
he'd observed, Roz wasn't the casual kind of girl.

Pierre entered the restaurant and stood just inside its
doors. This was one of his favorite times, being there early,
alone, before the rush, where he could plan, dream and
create new dishes without being interrupted. He walked
into the kitchen, rolled up his sleeves and gathered the
items to try out the first of two new signature dishes. He

gathered an armful of spices, fresh herbs, carrots, garlic and the Louisianan cook's holy trinity—onions, green peppers and celery—and walked over to a long, immaculate, stainless steel counter to start a broth. For him cooking was like meditation, and he looked forward to at least an hour alone in the kitchen before either the sous chef or the prep cooks arrived.

"Hey, boss. What are you cooking?"

It was not meant to be. Pierre looked at his watch, and with a sigh turned to see Riviera, his second-in-command, toss his knife roll on the counter and head toward him.

"You're an hour early. What are you doing here?"

"Getting ready for a packed house and steady traffic, same as you. What's that?"

"I don't know yet. Since you're here, grab me a five-pound bag of crayfish from the freezer."

Riviera smiled with a lopsided boyishness that matched his easygoing strides as he walked to the freezer. From there he headed to one of several industry-sized sinks for a thorough thaw and wash. "You meant crawdads, right?"

"At a family boil in Oklahoma, where you're from? Sure, that'll work. But served in a restaurant of our caliber, and at our price, they're crayfish."

Riviera laughed. "Might as well go all the way and call them freshwater lobsters."

"Even better. Working on a name for this dish. I'll keep that in mind."

The day's pace was insane. But except for a few aching muscles, Pierre found the eighteen-hour day felt like eight. He left the kitchen, went through a side door and walked around to the front of the building.

"Hey, man." He and Buddha exchanged a handshake. "You're out?"

"Finally. It's been a long day. How's everything out here?"

"You know how I do it. Everything's under control. Look, Easy, I really appreciate you giving me this job, man."

"You're clearly the best one for it. Who knew that I'd need someone like you here? But with the crowds and the VIPs coming in…it all worked out."

"My lady is looking for a larger apartment. With the family expanding, we need the room."

"It's about time to welcome the little one, huh?"

"Less than a month."

"Another one of our employee's wife is pregnant, too. Hope nothing's in the water."

"Keep the snake out and you don't have to worry."

Pierre laughed. His phone rang. "Alright, Buddha, be safe." Walking across the street to his SUV, he tapped the face and held the cell to his ear. "Hey, Lizzy!"

"Dang, brother! It's about time you answered your phone!"

"I know, baby girl. It's been crazy over here. I apologize. How's school?"

"It's been crazy over *here*."

Laughing, Pierre got into his car, switched to Bluetooth and pulled out of the parking lot.

"I'm trying to get through by December, so I doubled up on a couple classes."

"Is that affecting your grades?"

"It's affecting my sanity."

"Remember, you'll only get what I promised you by maintaining that 3.8."

"Brother, a white 560 with custom chrome is my computer screenshot. That's what helps get me through all these hours of studying."

"I'm proud of you, baby girl."

"You helped make it happen. The scholarship helped but I would have had to work my way through college if you weren't famous."

"Shut up with that."

"I had a copy of *NO Beat* on my bed. My roommate saw your picture and lost her mind."

"There were pictures with it?"

"Yeah, you didn't read the article?"

"The writer sent me a link to it. I never saw the paper."

"There were just a few. The Chow Channel, Intense Energy, and one of you and Marc."

Pierre frowned. "Me and Marc?"

"Uh-huh. In the New Orleans kitchen."

"Hmm."

"I like that writer, though, and the series she did to recognize the anniversary. This week's article was so moving, inspirational, but hard to read."

"Why?"

"It was about this guy who went missing during the storm. How it took his family a while to find him and how hard it was on them when he died. He was an athlete, headed for the pros. Like the family's golden boy, and then they found him and the dream was over."

"That sounds pretty sad, Liz."

"It was, but how the family has honored his memory is what was so inspiring. They have a scholarship in his name and a bunch of other stuff. The mother said that as hard as it was to know he was gone, finding his body gave them closure. It made me think of Mom…"

Pierre had spent years training himself not to think about her. It had been the only way he made it without losing his mind.

"Do you think about her, brother?"

"Not really."

"You don't wonder what happened?"

"I know what happened. And so do you. You just don't want to accept it."

"I know. The article said that dozens, maybe hundreds of people that went missing were never found. Roz, the writer, is dedicated to helping people get closure. There was no mention of Mom in your article. Why not?"

"The way I live life is letting the past stay in the past. Mom's not here. What else does anyone need to know?"

"It's just so weird without a body or jewelry or anything to say that she ever was here, let alone is now gone. I've been talking to my therapist about it and she suggested that maybe it's time we officially lay her to rest. Have a memorial or something to mark that she lived and she died, have it officially declared, and then move on. If I put something like that together, will you come?"

"Sure, Lizzy. If that will help you put the past behind you…"

The call ended, but not Pierre's thoughts about Alana LeBlanc, the woman who'd said she would meet them in Houston and then disappeared. That betrayal had shaped his view of women, had prevented him from ever having a genuine relationship. From the time he was fifteen years old, he'd never met a girl he felt he could trust. Hearing that part of Roz's focus was on the missing from Katrina put her questions and comments about his mom in a whole new light. Was there an ulterior motive to her interest in him? Could she be trusted?

Pierre didn't know, and wasn't sure he wanted to find out.

Chapter 12

Roz had convinced herself that Pierre not calling was probably best for them both. Strange as it seemed, though, she missed him. Thought about him. Wanted to talk to him and see how he was. So after a week had gone by, Roz put an end to the waiting game or standoff or whatever it was, and gave him a call.

"Hey, Pierre."

"Roz, what's up?"

"I called to see what you were doing, if you were in town."

"I'm here."

"I'm heading over to Ma's. Want to join me?"

"When are you going to be there?"

"I'm leaving right now."

"I'll meet you there."

Roz arrived first and was pleasantly surprised to see several tables taken. With few cars around when she'd pulled up, she assumed the customers lived nearby, and thought how cool it was that people like them, like herself, had kept Ma in business for at least twenty years. She walked over to one of the empty tables, waved at Ma as she passed the kitchen door.

A few minutes later Ma came out swinging a familiar red pail. "Hey there, lady."

"Hey, Ma." Roz stood up to hug her. "See you almost have a full house tonight."

"It's been like this for a couple weeks now. I don't know what's going on." Ma leaned in, lowered her voice. "They may be in the doghouse, their women mad and refusing to cook."

Only now did Roz notice that besides her and Ma there was only one other woman in the room.

"Whatever it is, I'm glad business is booming."

Ma set the pail on the table. "Where's that tall drink of water you brought with you the other day? The one who fancies himself a chef."

Roz smiled. "Pierre, that's his name. And actually, he's on his way."

"That's your man, right?"

"We're just friends."

Ma gave her a look. "Child, I've been on the earth too long for a lie like that to get by me."

"It's not a lie. We are not a couple."

"Why not? Are you crazy? You don't get a man like that in your crosshairs and not pull the trigger. You hear me?"

"Yes, ma'am."

"You need me to sprinkle a love potion on his food?"

"Ma, you're a mess!" Roz pulled out a crawfish and snapped the head. "I think whatever seasoning you've been using all this time is fine."

By the time Pierre arrived, the pail was almost empty and crawfish shells littered the newspaper-covered table.

"I see you started without me," he said in greeting, as he leaned over and gave her a casual hug.

"The thought when I started was to only eat a couple and the next thing I knew…this happened?"

"I understand."

His eyes caressed her as he settled into the plastic chair, in a way that caused moisture in private places. In that moment, Roz knew how the evening would end.

"How have you been? Wait, let me answer that. Busy?"

"How'd you guess?"

"Didn't I read somewhere that Beyoncé came through your place?"

Pierre nodded.

"Dude, you are in rarified air. Was she as nice as she appears to be on talk shows and stuff?"

"Even nicer. I've met a lot of celebrities, and it's funny how those who should be humble are the most egotistical, and someone like her, a triple, quadruple threat, is one of the most gracious people I've ever met."

"That's so nice to hear. I've always admired her music, her work. Now I like her even more."

"Hey, good-looking." Ma set a pail in front of Pierre. "These are yours and yours alone. Because somebody ate all of the ones I brought out earlier."

Roz looked around. "I wonder who?"

"Thanks, Ma." Pierre glanced around in turn. "You've got a crowd tonight. Are you poaching some of my customers?"

"No, baby. I'm just serving the kind of food that you can't get nowhere else."

Pierre watched Ma confidently walk away. "I love that woman."

"She's pretty amazing."

"Someone feels that way about you."

Roz's heart skipped a beat. "Who?"

"My sister."

"Oh, really?" Roz succeeded in keeping her smile in place, chiding herself for the expectation that the thought came from him.

"Yes. I didn't know the story you wrote on me was part of a series on Katrina."

"The title was 'Hurricane Katrina Survivors: Where Are They Now?' That didn't give you a clue?"

"Alright, woman." He laughed along with her. "Clearly,

I didn't pay close enough attention. My sister did. She read the whole series and was quite impressed."

"Thank you to your sister."

"I'll let her know. She said this was an anniversary piece or something?"

Roz nodded. "I do something every year. Most of the rest of the world has forgotten. I write for those affected in a way that they will never forget."

"I thought you were gone when the storm hit."

"I was."

"Yet you're so passionate. Other than being from here, why are you so involved?"

"I lost someone very special. My best friend's brother."

"I'm sorry."

"Me, too."

"He lived in the area that got flooded?"

Roz shook her head. "He didn't, but a friend of his did. The irony of it all is that his family didn't know he was over here. They didn't know where he was exactly, but assumed that he was with a cousin who lives in Baton Rouge. That's where he'd been the previous weekend, and as far as the family knew, he still was. So when they decided to leave the city and go to a hotel, they left a voice mail on his phone and that was it.

"They left on Saturday night and didn't try to contact him again until Sunday. Couldn't get him. Called the cousin, who said he'd left with a couple friends, some guys on his high school's football team. So again the Powells weren't overly worried. Aaron was a great guy. He was smart, responsible. He wasn't into drugs or gangs or anything like that. He lived, ate and slept football. And girls. Aaron loved the ladies. And they loved him back. But he had goals and was laser focused. Go to Grambling State. Play for the Saints. That was it. Then Monday came…"

"And the levees broke."

Roz's head shot up. "You remember, the twenty-ninth."

"I remember."

"That's right, because you were in it, too. With the sister who read my series, and your mom."

"My sister's name is Lisette."

"I know you had to grow up fast and life was hard, which is probably why you don't want to talk about it, but…things could have turned out differently. Be glad you made it on that bus."

"By Monday night, when we'd still not heard from Aaron, we all panicked and started calling the friends he'd left with. Days went by. It was crazy. Then we connected with one of them—I can't even remember the crazy way we finally made contact—but he told us that Aaron and Jackson, Aaron's best friend, had gone to help Jackson's sister evacuate. She lived in the heart of the area that the world saw underwater. None of us wanted to believe that he didn't get out. But after days went by, and then a week…we knew."

"You ever find him?"

Roz nodded. "Aaron was my brother, basically. I've known Stefanie and the Powells since I was eight years old and, being an only child, I invited myself into their family and refused to leave. They were so distraught that they couldn't handle the process of searching, but the journalist in me kicked in and I became obsessed with knowing what happened. So, yes, it took a few weeks, but we were able to…say goodbye."

Ma brought out a new dish and the conversation turned. But in that prior conversation, something shifted. Roz could feel it. And later, when Pierre invited her to his home, she knew for sure.

Chapter 13

Pierre hadn't intended to invite Roz over. But after sharing her heart the way she did, it felt natural. He couldn't see sending her home alone. He didn't want to be alone either. Hearing her talk about Aaron stirred up feelings Pierre hadn't acknowledged in years. He thought about his sister's desire for closure. He'd accepted their mother's death years ago. But if a formal memorial would help Lisette…

Pierre lived in a freestanding, three-story townhome, one of very few newly constructed buildings near the French Quarter, in the Marigny neighborhood. Its exquisite design included an outdoor living space with a fireplace and kitchen, a plunge pool and a balcony overlooking Cabrini Park. High ceilings, white walls, dark hardwood floors and marble lent a modern masculinity that fitted Pierre's personality perfectly. The only room he'd redesigned was the kitchen. Naturally.

His other favorite room was where he headed. The master suite, which took up much of the third floor. He drew a bath, lit vanilla-scented candles and put on his favorite album by Najee. He was back downstairs, checking out his wine collection, when Roz called.

"I'm here."

"Are you around back?"

"No, how do I get back there?"

He told her and then walked through the house to meet her.

She pulled in next to his SUV and got out, looking around.

"You know what's crazy? I've seen this place. Didn't pay it that much attention, but I've driven by and noticed it because this used to be an empty lot. It looks rather plain on the outside. No one would ever imagine this beautiful courtyard. Thanks for inviting me to your home. That makes me feel special."

They hugged.

"I've missed you," he whispered against her hair.

"Me, too. There was something so special for me about the time in New York. Magical, really."

"So you believe in magic, huh?"

Roz nodded as he wrapped his arm around her shoulders and led her inside. Then he hugged her from behind, his breath hot and wet against her temple. "Let's try and make it happen again."

They shared a glass of wine, a little small talk, but it became clear what was on both their minds.

The first kiss was a whisper, containing hints of promises—excitement, passion, heat. Roz offered it naturally, organically, as a Band-Aid for the pain that seemed to seep from Pierre's soul when he told of being wrenched away from New Orleans. An ache she felt when sharing Aaron's fate. But an electrical ardor ignited the kiss, taking it from comfort to something else altogether. He swiped his tongue across her lips, used it to ask, beg, demand that she open up so he could pour lust inside her mouth. Coat her heart, set her body on fire. That's the only explanation Roz's muddled mind could grasp as she pressed her body against him, feeling that even the thin layers of clothing that prevented flesh-to-flesh contact was too much distance. Somewhere far off in the distance, warning bells sounded.

Roz, stop, before you get hurt again.

But then his lips separated from hers, brushed across

her cheek to her neck and shoulder. His hand caressed the other shoulder before moving down to her sleeveless T-shirt, then beneath it, to a nipple. Fondled it, tweaked it, through a sheer mesh bra. Like an angel on the other shoulder, her body spoke then, in a voice that was louder than the one that warned.

Just enjoy it. Let yourself go.

She listened to that angel. Turned her body toward him to provide easier access. Ran her hands across broad shoulders and muscled arms that caused an errant thought: *Guess Guido's Gym was a good fit.*

His lips skimmed the top of her shirt before he lifted his head to once again claim her waiting lips. His tongue slipped inside, hers welcomed the duel. He tasted of ginger and mint. Of exhilaration and abandon. The taste remained as he began a journey similar to the one in New York, only it began from the top this time. He alternated between soft and wet kisses, licks and nips over her neck and shoulders, down to her breasts. He cupped her average-sized mounds in his hands, licked the dark nipples until they were hard and erect. Kisses followed the trail forged by his hands. Down her stomach, over her hips, across her buttocks, outlining its crease.

The intensity of his loving aroused Roz almost beyond control. It was too much pleasure for her alone to enjoy. She shifted her body even as he assailed her, wrapped her hand around the base of his gorgeous shaft and gave to him what he'd given to her. Over and again she circled his tip with her tongue, rubbed its length with her hands, drew his girth into her warmth. Smiled as he swerved his hips, thrust deeper inside her and moaned. It felt good to know that she pleased him. Made her feel sexy and powerful to feel the goose bumps on his buttocks and hear his sighs. But moments later, when he ordered her to her knees and positioned himself behind her, there was no doubt as to who wielded the most powerful weapon, who was in control. Roz gladly surrendered herself to relentless pounding that he would alternately soothe with his tongue.

Having experienced him in New York, she thought she was ready. But when he shifted and hit a spot inside her that had never been touched, she reached a climax that left her shaking and sobbing. After, lying on their sides, she wrapped her arms around his neck and held on tightly, afraid that if she didn't she would float right out of this world.

Chapter 14

Roz's body tingled, her lower lips still quivering from the orgasmic explosion. *What in the world just happened?* She felt light-headed, couldn't tell whether her ears were ringing or Najee was holding a note with his sax. It felt as though her entire body had been shot weightless into another galaxy before floating back down. Bones so relaxed they felt like lead. Heart beating, only because it could do so on its own. Beside her, Pierre's breathing became slow and even. Finally, long moments later, he turned and pulled her into his arms, pulled a cover over them both and spooned.

"That was amazing," he murmured against her temple.

"Hmm." Several more minutes passed. "I'm in trouble."

"Why, baby?"

"Because your body is a drug and I am addicted. Someone call 9-1-1."

Pierre chuckled. "Don't worry about it, baby. Whenever you need a shot, I'm here."

The music switched from Najee to Earl Klugh. As Roz regained energy she began to rock, softly, slowly, against Pierre's body. Time passed. Roz felt him shift onto his back.

"Roz, are you sleep?"

"No."

Pierre remained quiet. Roz turned over to face him, repositioned the pillow to support her neck. She watched him, waited for what he had to say. Placed a hand on his chest and stroked it.

"Remember when you interviewed me the first time, and asked questions about Katrina?"

"Yes."

"And I didn't want to talk about it?"

Roz nodded.

"The reason is because my sister and I had happen to us the same thing that happened to your friend's brother, Aaron."

"You lost someone?"

Pierre nodded. "We never found her body."

"Who was it?" Roz asked, her voice barely above a whisper.

A long time went by, so much that she wasn't sure he'd tell her. But finally he did. "My mom."

The shock of his answer caused Roz to sit up. "Oh, no. Pierre, I am so sorry."

"Yeah, me, too. It tore me up, liked to have killed me if you want to know the truth. After that I closed a part of myself off. It's hard for me to open up and trust and share. I found myself wanting to do that with you. At the time I thought it was because you were a journalist and were trained to extract information. You might be," he added, his eyes shifting toward her. "But hearing the story you shared at Ma's made me realize that it wasn't just your technique or a style or anything like that. It's because you understood the incident in a way that only those who were affected by it can understand. Because you went through it, too."

"Yeah, I did. One of the most painful experiences of my life." She moved her hand from his chest to his arm, offering encouraging caresses as she waited for him to continue.

"Back then I didn't know where to start that process, or who to ask. My cousins weren't helpful. The aunt we stayed with and my mom weren't all that close. She had her own problems. It was like, 'She's gone. Life goes on. Work it out.' In order to do that I just shut down that part of my life. Didn't discuss it with anyone, not even Lizzy. Which looking back was really hard on her. She's in therapy now and wants to have a memorial for Mom. Feels it will help bring closure."

"I think formally acknowledging a situation and celebrating that person's life does help shift things for the better. Helps you remember the good times, to pay attention to all of the years that they lived instead of the one day that they stopped living."

"Maybe I'll have my sister call you, and you can give her some ideas. Would that be okay?"

"I'd love to help."

He nodded.

"What was your mom's name?"

"Alana." He spelled it. "Alana LeBlanc."

This time it was Roz who reached out and spooned next to Pierre. "Thanks for sharing your story with me."

"You're welcome."

There was no official announcement, but later Roz would realize that in this moment they became a couple. Just like that.

Chapter 15

Pierre's story touched Roz deeply. She could only imagine how it must have been for him to open up about his mother. She'd felt the kind of pain that went with having someone there one moment and gone the next. Even more troubling was the fact they'd never found her. For the Powells, not knowing Aaron's whereabouts had been excruciating, and while his death left a void that could never be filled, Roz remembered the peace that came with finding him, honoring him and giving him a proper goodbye. Most people called it closure. Roz called it clarity. The identification erased the question marks, put the story of what really happened in place of imaginations run wild. It didn't take long for her to decide that she wanted to do the same for Pierre and Lisette. She had access to sources beyond the general public, and knew that dozens of victims identified through DNA had not been claimed. It was a haunting, tragic process, one she felt Pierre and his sister did not need to know about. At least until she had answers that could hopefully bring them peace and clarity.

The week after the magical night at Pierre's house, Roz reached out to her contact in public records. "Flint, Roz Arnaud."

"Roz! It's been a while. How are you?"

"Busy but good. You?"

"Working on my retirement."

"You wish. You're what, five years older than me. So you're going to hang it up at thirty-five, huh?"

"If I can get one of the plans in place."

"What kind of plan can retire you that early?"

"One called Super Lotto or Powerball."

They both cracked up.

"Whew, I'm glad you're joking. You'd be a hard connection to replace. A connection with connections."

"Don't worry. I'm not going anywhere. What can I do for you?"

"Got a missing person. Katrina."

"Whoa."

"Yeah, I know. Figured we could start with the DNA pool. If we don't find it there, run it through your other sources."

"Okay, shoot."

"Alana LeBlanc." Roz spelled it for him.

"Date of birth."

Roz shared what she'd pulled from public records.

"Alright, give me a few days. Hit me back."

"I owe you one. Thanks, Flint."

As Roz rode the waves of new love, summer became fall. Pierre's schedule was as crazy as ever and she was busy, too. Even so, they saw each other anytime or day that their schedules allowed. When her phone rang at 2:00 a.m. Roz wasn't surprised to roll over and see Pierre's number on the screen.

"Hey."

"You're already sexy. It's not necessary to try and sound like that."

"I'm not." Roz cleared her throat. "You woke me up."

"Oh, baby, I'm sorry."

"Right. Sorry not sorry."

"Something like that. I just got off work."

"Oh, okay. So did you wake me up to chat or was there something else on your mind?"

"Probably the same thing that's on yours. Hold that thought…"

Twenty minutes later Pierre was in her shower, looking luscious and in Roz's opinion a bit out of place in her frilly, white, pink and purple master bath. It was the one place in the home she'd allowed her girlie side to shine. The pastels, and floral borders, a throwback feature that fit perfectly in a bathroom over a hundred fifty years old. The atmosphere changed, though, when Pierre strolled out, all muscle and manliness, wrapped in a hot-pink towel that gripped his hips and covered his treasure. Not for long. Roz reached for the towel and pulled back her top sheet in one long motion. Invited him into her bed, into her heat, giving as good as she got. Little conversation. There was no need. All the talking was done with tongues and hands, moaning and sighs. Unlike that first night in New York that felt rushed and preoccupied, tonight was slow and easy. He gripped her thigh, held her leg in the air and set up a rhythmic thrusting that sent her over the edge again and again. Until she shook with the ecstasy of it all. Until once again there were tears.

Afterward, he pulled her into his arms and smoothed down her damp hair.

"Baby, sucking on you is better than sucking on crayfish," he whispered against her pulsing temple.

Roz burst out laughing. "It's a good thing I'm a swamp girl and know how much you love them, because otherwise that's not at all romantic, babe."

"No?"

"No, it's gross."

"Then can I say you're my side dish, better than a pile of dirty rice?"

"Sure," Roz cooed, reaching down to squeeze his

manhood. "Because this right here is definitely my main course."

"Hmm."

They became quiet, wrapped in each other's arms with nothing but the sounds of the night between them.

After several minutes, he cocked his head toward the ceiling. "Is that rain?"

"Yes." Roz snuggled closer and rested her head on his chest.

"Sounds strange."

"It's the roof. Flat seam metal by the solar panels."

"Solar panels? Here, in New Orleans?"

"Why not? The sun does shine here."

"I guess." He shifted the pillow and rested against it. "I used to like the sound of rain."

He said it softly. As if to himself.

"Before Katrina?" She felt his nod against her curls. "Speaking of, I was talking to Lisette about a memorial for your mom and I learned you lost your grandmother, too?"

"Unfortunately."

"Babe, why didn't you... Never mind."

"Outside of my sister, I've never talked about it." His eyes fell on her. "Until you."

They listened to the rain. When he spoke again it was so low that she shifted her head to hear him. "My grandmother didn't want to leave. She'd lived here her whole life. As far as I know there were only one or two times she left the state. Mom told her we needed to go, showed her the mayor on TV ordering a complete evacuation. It was getting worse and worse, so Mom told us to grab a few things, told Grand-Mère she was taking us to the bus station and to be ready when she got back."

Roz felt his shrug as he murmured, "Never saw them again."

"Pierre, my heart hurts for you." She thought about Flint, and hoped when she called him in a couple days, he'd have news. "That you and Lisette have done so well speaks to the strength you both have. Especially your sister. She's so positive and bubbly. No one would look at her and know what she's been through."

"She adjusted to the changes better than me, that's for sure. The transition in Texas was easier for her. I was glad about that."

"Why do you think that was?"

"Her personality, definitely, all the things you just said. Plus she was younger. The cousins her age embraced her right away, were glad to have somebody else in their clique."

"And you?"

"A bunch of testosterone-driven teens that you don't really know and never liked in the first place? Them mistaking my quiet nature for believing I was better than them? It made me retreat even more. Once I started school, it really blew up. I liked school, liked to go to there, was popular. All traits frowned upon in that part of town. I got teased and then threatened for not hitting the street and engaging in certain activities. I stumbled into Marc and New Orleans right on time."

Roz glanced at the clock. It was almost four. She snuggled up to Pierre and tried to ignore the fact that she'd get up in just a few hours. Pierre's story and her desire to bring them clarity made sleep elusive. Which was why she was awake when Pierre turned to tell her, "Babe, I think I like the rain again."

Chapter 16

Roz waited until the end of the week, then texted Flint. He hadn't found anything and said to check back in another week. But the following Monday, just into October, Flint caught her just as she was leaving *NO Beat*.

"Hey, Flint!"

"Hey."

"Hold on a second. I'm almost to my car." She got in and started it up to activate the Bluetooth. "Alright, guy, what do you have for me?"

"If what I found is accurate, not what you're expecting."

Roz's heart dropped. She knew the chances were slim that Pierre and Lisette's mom would be one of those identified through DNA.

"It's okay. I knew it was a long shot. The more time passes, the less likely those missing will ever be found. I appreciate you taking the time, though, so the next time I see you, drinks will still be on me."

"Hold on, Roz. I didn't say that I didn't find anything. I said it probably wasn't what you were expecting."

"So you did find DNA identified as Alana LeBlanc?"

"No, I found a person named Lana Stern, who matches the information I collected regarding LeBlanc."

"I don't understand. What are you saying?"

"I'm saying that there's no DNA match for the name you gave me because that woman isn't dead. Alana Le-Blanc, now Lana Stern, is alive."

Roz had to pull over.

"Flint, are you sure?"

"I've scanned what I came across and will email it to you."

Roz still couldn't process what he had told her. Katrina had happened in 2005. So, what, Alana had had been in hiding for more than a decade? For Roz, the answer could only be "no way."

Still, the journalist in her would not let it go. "Send over what you've got, Flint. I'll be in touch."

By the time she arrived home, Flint's scans were in her email. She printed them out, becoming more confused and uncomfortable with every one she read. She wanted to talk to Pierre, but knew there was no way she'd ignite that kind of hope without concrete proof. Roz studied the documents gained by Flint's research team, including a marriage license for an Alana LeBlanc to a Bernard L. Stern. Could these have somehow been created before 2005? There had to be a logical explanation. That she'd survived Katrina made no sense. All night she grappled with what he had uncovered. By the next morning, she'd decided what to do.

She walked into Andy's office and closed the door. "Morning, Andy."

"Arnaud. What's going on? Don't tell me you're leaving to work for the Brass."

"Why would I do that?"

"You haven't heard? Ginny quit to join their PR department."

"No, I hadn't. When is she leaving?"

"She's already gone. Said she couldn't give notice, that they needed her right away. I couldn't match what they offered so she switched teams."

"I hate to hear that, Andy, especially with what I've come to talk about. I need a couple days off. Emergency."

"Why? What's going on?"

"I'd rather not say."

"This is business, or personal?"

"A little bit of both."

"I suppose you want this on *NO Beat*'s account?"

"I can buy my ticket. What's important is that I go right away. Like tomorrow."

"You've got to give me some idea of what's going on."

"Okay. I have it on good authority that someone with high-profile connections may have, for lack of a better description, faked their death."

"Oh, come on."

"Exactly my reaction. But I've seen enough documentation to fly to LA on my own dime if I have to and either confirm or deny what was given. If I have this information today, the competition may have it tomorrow."

"*NO Beat* will take care of your ticket. The only thing I ask is that once the information is confirmed, that you give me the lead on this story."

"Fair enough."

The next day, Roz arrived in LAX and texted the Uber she'd booked for the day to drive her around. The female driver wasn't far. Having only carry-on luggage, Roz was out of the airport and heading to the valley and the address she had for Lana Stern within ten minutes.

Their destination was forty-five minutes away. The driver was chatty, the scenery grand. Roz was only vaguely aware of her surroundings, however. Her mind was consumed with meeting Alana, Lana, whomever, and getting the story. She'd purposely not given much thought to the process. Some of her best work had come when flying by the seat of her pants. But the closer they got to Sherman Oaks, the city in San Fernando Valley where the woman lived, the less sure she was that a surprise visit to someone's home was the best idea. Having a door slammed in her face, or even worse, not even opened, and the trip would be over. The opportunity lost. She needed a strategy, and maybe an accomplice. Leaning forward, she decided to feel her driver out.

"Peyton, right?"

"Yes."

"Are you familiar with Sherman Oaks?"

Peyton nodded. "Basically. I've lived in the Valley all my life. Grew up in Van Nuys."

"Is that near the address I gave you?"

"A couple miles give or take, depending on where you're going in either city. But Sherman Oaks is more expensive. Million dollar homes and stuff."

"Hmm. Do a lot of celebrities live there?"

"There are celebrities all over. Sherman Oaks has a large Jewish population. Older people, established. Not as diverse as Van Nuys or other areas in the Valley. I'd say it's probably 75 percent white."

"I've traveled here to surprise…someone…" Roz hesitated, not wanting to lie, but knowing that the entire truth could not be told either.

"A friend?"

"Yes." That might become true. From what she saw and what Peyton said, Roz felt the chances were slim that whoever she met was down on her luck. Clearly, she wasn't homeless. In fact, as they exited on Ventura Boulevard and she took in the surroundings, Roz assumed that if this were indeed Alana LeBlanc she was doing okay, maybe doing great.

"It's been a really long time since she's been back to where we grew up. I'm not sure just walking up to her house is the best idea."

"Why not? I mean, if you guys are old friends…"

"It's a long story, but let's just say I'm not sure how I'll be received. It's a meeting that needs to happen. I just think it might go better…maybe a public place… You know what? You're right. Just drive to the address as originally planned. Whether I'm invited in or the door slams in my face, I've tried. Right?"

"Right."

"Just be sure and wait for me in the drive."

"Of course."

"With the car running."

Peyton glanced back "Are you serious?"

"No." *Yes.* "Just kidding."

Magnolia, the street where Alana lived, was a wide boulevard lined with tall palms and shorter trees shading homes of different styles and sizes. A middle to upper-middle area, Roz deduced as they continued down the street. Bottom line, there was no way to tell from her surroundings what type of woman she'd be meeting. Roz sat back, took deep breaths and hummed "Que sera."

They reached the address Flint had provided. That the house looked average made Roz feel a little more comfortable. Before she could get inside her own head she reached for the door handle. "I don't think this will take longer than thirty minutes, okay?"

Peyton pulled out her cell phone. "Take your time. I'll be here."

Roz was all business as she exited the car and walked to the front door. Mere seconds passed before, through the colored glass blocks, she made out someone approaching.

The door opened. It was not Lana Stern.

"Hello. May I help you?"

"Yes, good morning. I'm here to see Mrs. Stern."

"Do you have an appointment?"

"No, but I have some important, confidential information that I've come all the way from New Orleans to deliver."

"And your name?"

"Rosalyn Arnaud." She reached into her briefcase-styled handbag and provided a business card.

The middle-aged Latina's face remained neutral as, with a slight nod, she said, "Wait one moment, please."

Roz stepped back, but not before seeing something that was even more unsettling than the home's beautiful and immaculate interior, and what appeared to be a housekeeper or personal assistant. A tall, pretty girl who looked to be in her teens. If this was indeed Alana, did she have another child?

Before she could process that possibility, the woman who'd answered the door returned. "Come in, please."

Roz was then ushered into a well-appointed sitting room.

"Could I get you something to drink? Tea? Water?"

"No, thank you."

The woman left as quietly as she'd come. Too nervous to sit, Roz took in the beautiful artwork that lined the wall. Several minutes went by before the door opened again. After a fortifying deep breath, she turned around.

"Mrs. Stern? Lana? Hi, I'm Rosalyn Arnaud." She walked forward smiling, her arm outstretched, and took in a tall, attractive woman with flawless skin and Pierre's eyes.

Her handshake was half-hearted, tentative. "Have a seat."

Roz sat on a couch as Lana directed, while she sat on one of two straight-back Queen Anne chairs that flanked a side table inlaid with what looked to be gold.

"Why are you here?"

Direct. No nonsense. Roz liked that.

"I'm here to confirm whether or not you, Lana Stern, were formerly Alana LeBlanc from New Orleans, Louisiana."

She watched Lana's eyes widen slightly, her posture, already rigid, become even more erect. Lana remained silent.

"As my card indicates, I'm a journalist working for the *New Orleans Beat*, better known as *NO Beat*. A few months ago the celebrity chef Pierre LeBlanc opened a restaurant in the city. It was a huge deal, a sold-out success from before the doors opened. Every media outlet in the city and many nationally all wanted to do a feature on him, *NO Beat* included. I got the interview and because everyone else wrote about the restaurant and the food, I decided to write about the man behind the restaurant. It was from that angle that I learned of his journey to the kitchen. The one that started when Hurricane Katrina drove him and his sister to Houston, and caused his mother and grandmother to disappear."

Roz watched as Alana's eyes began to blink rapidly. She swallowed several times. Turned and looked out the window. "How did you find me?"

"I'm right? You are Pierre and Lisette's mother, Alana LeBlanc?"

"How did you find me?" Her voice remained low, but carried the authority of someone used to giving orders and having them followed.

"A friend of mine is a PI. I don't know the specifics or who his sources are, but after carefully researching the limited information I gave him he came back with… the name you use now…an address and a phone number."

"Why didn't you call? Who do you think you are, to just show up on my doorstep asking questions like you have the right?"

"I didn't think you'd take my call, or stay on the phone once you found out the reason I was calling. I felt that if that happened, I would have tipped my hand and been closed off to the truth forever."

"Did Pierre send you here?"

"He knows nothing about this visit."

Lana frowned. "Then I ask the question once again. Why are you here?"

"For the truth, Mrs. Stern. Alana, if I may."

"Lana."

"Okay."

"If Pierre didn't send you, what does any of this matter to you?"

"Look, I come here with no hidden agenda. No judgment. No idea of what, if anything, will come out of this visit.

"When I interviewed Pierre, he evaded the topics of family and Hurricane Katrina, I found that curious, puzzling. The journalist in me felt that it wasn't just because he was a private guy or anything like that. I had this nagging feeling that there was more to his story. On top of that, like many New Orleanians, I have a special connection with Katrina. I wasn't there when it hit. But my best friend's brother disappeared in the flood. It was three weeks before his body was identified in a massive… Anyway, I became especially interested in stories like that. People who'd gone missing or are still missing. For many, interest in Katrina and how it affected New Orleans receded with the floodwater. Most people don't know or care that even now, today, some areas show little change. So many lives were affected. My life. Pierre's life." She paused and added, "Your life."

Lana rose abruptly, walked over to an ornate armoire that housed a mini bar. She reached for a tumbler and poured two fingers of a brown liquor, then turned to Roz. "Scotch?"

"Oh, no, thank you."

Lana nodded, returned to her seat and slowly sipped the drink as her eyes stared beyond the room and into yesterday.

"I had a troubled childhood, very difficult. Details I won't share. When home became unbearable I ran away. Looked for love outside the house. Got pregnant. Went to work.

"The signs of Mom's MS began about two years before Lisette was born, and it fell on me to take care of her. There was no discussion. I was her only child so it was what I would do. I resented it, greatly, and wasn't always kind in my treatment of her. When the streets flooded and after putting the kids on the bus, I waded through mucky water to find my mother in her wheelchair, wedged between a couch and a heavy table that had floated on top of her. Something in me snapped."

Lana drained the tumbler. "I went crazy. For sure. Ended up at East Hospital. That's where I met Bernie."

"Bernard Stern?"

"Yes, my husband. He was one of many doctors who flew in and volunteered their services. Checked me out. Bandaged me up. Then they transferred me to Community Care."

"The psychiatric hospital."

Lana nodded. Her posture changed, became somewhat relaxed as she spoke of her husband. "The next day I looked up and there was Dr. Stern to see me. I had no idea why. I'd not uttered a word since finding my mom like that, which is how I ended up over there. But he acted like my madness was the most normal thing. He talked nonstop, about everything. Himself, his practice, life in LA. It sounded like paradise. Several days passed before I realized he wasn't visiting me in the role of doctor but of a man interested in finding out more about me. I couldn't believe it. When he asked if I had children, I said no."

Lana looked directly at Roz for the first time. "I don't know why. The lie just came out, almost on its own."

She looked away again. "The day I decided to tell him the truth is the day he asked me to come home with him. Two weeks later, I was on a plane. There never seemed to be a good time after that."

"Did you think about them?"

"I couldn't. Not at first. Bernie set me up with a therapist and that's when the healing began. That's when I told myself that when the time was right I'd tell him about the kids, and go get them, and we'd all live happily ever after. Then I… Then things changed."

"You got pregnant?"

"How did you—"

"Just now, as the door opened, I saw a pretty young lady cross the hall and just assumed…"

"Yes, that's our daughter. Totally unplanned. Life happened and years passed… I searched for them on the internet, began tracking their lives. Like a stalker. Lisette is so beautiful and smart. Pierre…by the time I was mentally strong enough, I felt I had no right to interrupt what had become their lives. But know this. I never, ever, stopped loving them. I loved them enough to let them go."

"Lana, I can't put myself in your shoes. But you've got two kids who think you're dead!"

"I've told myself everything you're thinking and many things you can't comprehend. I've watched them blossom. Know all about their lives. Can you imagine what it's like to have a handsome, successful, celebrity son like Pierre and not be able to let him know I'm alive? And not just because he's a celebrity. He could work at a gas station and I'd feel the same way. I just can't see how to reenter their lives."

"By ending this lie, and returning."

They talked for another half hour. Roz shared her plans to let Pierre know what she'd discovered, and got Lana's permission to pass on her number should he or Lisette want to call. Roz left in an even bigger state of disbelief than she'd been in during her phone call with Flint. All she could think of was how Pierre would accept the news. When she'd encouraged him to get clarity about what happened to his mother, this was not what she'd had in mind.

Chapter 17

On Friday, Roz woke up early. If asked, she would have said she felt "some kind of way." It was an emotion, or several, that she couldn't describe. She guessed it was the letdown after a whirlwind, eventful twenty-four hours, a time during which she hadn't gotten much sleep. The conversation she'd had with Lana Stern, Pierre's mom, had played like a nonstop loop in her head. What she'd shared was everything that made for a tragic yet captivating story. Disaster, loss, illness, love, sadness, regret.

And perhaps reunion?

Roz thought of Pierre. Her stomach lurched. How he and his sister would react was the missing piece to her tableau. From the few discussions she'd had with him about his mom, it could go either way. Would he be angry for her being alive all this time and just now reaching out? Or would he be happy and ready to write new chapters in their lives? She'd talk with him before discussing anything with Andy, or writing a single word for an article. She'd explain everything that had happened, and why she'd felt it necessary to vet the woman who claimed to be Pierre's mom before sharing what she'd learned. Pierre was a laid-back, even-keeled brother. Even with the unexplainable nervousness she felt, she believed he would understand and not have a problem with the story she'd write. This was an above the fold, breaking news story. If *NO Beat* didn't publish it, someone else eventually would.

Roz arrived at work and walked straight into Andy's

office. She closed the door, moved a stack of files off the only other chair in the room and sat down.

"Well?"

"I was able to confirm that someone assumed to be deceased is alive. But I can't tell you who it is yet. Not until I've had a chance to tell the family."

"That wasn't the deal."

"I'm going to talk to them tonight. By Monday, I'll have a write-up."

"You're being extremely protective about this. Is it one of your relatives?"

"No, but I know them. It's only right that they be the first ones to hear what I've learned."

"Of course, you won't reveal your source."

"Of course."

"But you're sure the information you received is authentic."

"One hundred percent."

"I'm going to go with my gut and trust you on this, Roz. I'll give you until noon on Monday. Then you need to let the editor-in-chief of the paper that pays your salary know exactly what's going on."

Roz left the office feeling nauseous. She tried to focus on a positive outcome. Yes, Pierre's mom had deceived him, but in her mind she was doing what was best. How many people got the chance to reconnect with a loved one they thought dead? Maybe Roz was freaking out about a scenario that wouldn't happen. While in this positive frame of mind, she called Pierre.

"Hey, babe, it's Roz. I know Fridays are crazy, but I really need to see you. I'm hoping to come over after you get off. It's important, so call me, okay?"

Roz returned to work, but after two hours of writing absolutely nothing that could be printed, she gave up the pretense and went to the gym. A two-hour workout helped her feel a little better and by the time she went home and stepped in a hot bath the whirlwind forty-eight hours with very little sleep finally caught up to her. She fell asleep in the tub, awoke to a tub of cold water and climbed naked into bed.

Later, when she checked her phone, there were messages from several people, including Stefanie. Roz would call them all later. Right now the only person she wanted to talk to was Pierre. While sipping a glass of wine, she received a text.

Headed home. Meet me there.

As always, Pierre's message caused her to smile. She hoped what she told him would eventually have the same effect.

Roz arrived at Pierre's and entered through an unlocked door. Within a second of seeing him all the calm she felt from the rest, workout and wine disappeared.

Pierre must have heard the door open. He came down the hall with arms outstretched. "Hello, beautiful."

"Hey." Roz welcomed his hug and wrapped her arms around his waist.

"Whoa, baby, what's this?"

"What?"

"Your body is tight, tense." He walked behind her, began massaging her neck. "I think I know what you need."

Roz felt faint, suffocating under the weight of what she'd come to tell Pierre. She stepped away from him and slowly turned around. "I have something to tell you."

Immediate concern showed on his face. "Are you pregnant?"

"No! I'm in shock but not because I'm pregnant. But I do have news. Let's sit down."

"You're starting to worry me, Roz." Pierre sat and pulled Roz down beside him. "What is it?"

"I did something that I thought would help you and Lisette have closure, or what I call clarity regarding your mom. I knew you guys hadn't been able to find out anything about her, and so I wanted to try and help you."

"Why are you so nervous, baby? That's not a bad thing. It touches me that you wanted to help."

"Yes, I'd done it with Aaron and other people, so I contacted my connections in public records and everything… There's no easy way to tell you this." Roz scooted closer to him and reached for his hands. "Pierre, your mom is alive."

Roz waited, watched to gauge his reaction. There wasn't much of one. He cocked his head as if trying to decipher a foreign language and then, as if slowly getting the interpretation, eased his hands out of hers.

"What?"

"I know it sounds crazy. My reaction was just like yours. Disbelief. I asked for all kinds of proof and even then had to research it for myself. I had to know for sure, before I said anything to you, that the information I had was authentic beyond a shadow of a doubt."

"No." Pierre fell back against the couch, then got up and began to pace. "There's no way either my mother or grandmother could have survived those waters. You saw the pictures. It was a raging river down there. I don't know what you saw and I know you probably want it to be true, but that's impossible."

"I met her."

Pierre rejoined her on the couch. "What do you mean, you met her?"

"I had some pretty solid proof that a woman formerly known as Alana LeBlanc was alive and living in Los Angeles. But like I said, I wouldn't breathe a word to you or

Lisette and set up any kind of false hope unless I had ir-refutable proof. So I flew to Los Angeles. I went to the address that my contact had given and I met this woman."

Roz took a breath and pulled out a picture. Her hands shook as she quietly passed it to Pierre. He took it, looking at her with an expression that she could not define. After a moment, he looked at the picture. Several seconds passed. He closed his eyes. His hand went slack. The picture fluttered soundlessly to the floor.

There was no need to ask if he was okay. Given what he'd just found out, there was no way he could be. Roz placed a gentle hand on his forearm. *I'm here for you, babe. I'm right here.*

Pierre stood abruptly, slowly walked from one end of the living room to the other. Crossed over to a set of French doors. Opened them and walked out.

A concerned Roz hurried out after him. "I can't imag-ine how you're feeling now. I know this is a lot to take in."

"I can't believe that's my…mother." His voice was barely audible, raspy with suppressed emotion.

Roz stood a couple feet behind him, wanting to make him feel better. Wanting to take away the pain.

"You saw her yesterday?"

Roz nodded. "I did. She lives in the San Fernando Val-ley in a city called Sherman Oaks."

"How did you find her?"

"Through a friend, a private investigator who I've used before. He has access to information and resources that are not available to the general public, and sometimes not even in the records of the coroner's office. Because I told him the circumstances surrounding her disappearance, he was surprised to get a hit through another set of records more recent than 2005. So he dug a little further and, needless to say, I was not expecting to hear what he told me. At all.

Even after hearing it and deciding to fly to LA, I thought I'd meet a woman with the same name as your mom, and even told my contact to keep looking for the records to confirm her passing." Roz felt yesterday's shock all over again. "Need to tell him to stop that search," she mumbled to herself.

Roz watched as a flurry of emotions ping-ponged across Pierre's face. She could imagine some of them. They'd been the ones she'd experienced herself. He looked over at the picture on the floor, finally went and picked it up. He stared at it for a long time.

"Come here," he finally said.

Roz walked over with arms outstretched. Pierre walked into her embrace. She imagined that he was crying, but when he stepped back a short time later, his eyes were dry. He took her hand and led her to the sofa.

"Sit down."

Roz sat at an angle that faced him.

"Tell me what happened."

She began telling an abbreviated version of what had unfolded after she'd knocked on Alana's door. "The doctor who'd treated her at East began visiting her at the mental hospital, every day, she said, and after a couple weeks invited her to go home with him."

"Did she lose her memory along with her mind? Did she have amnesia and forget she had kids?"

"Her plan was to come back for you guys at some point, but…"

"But what?"

Roz squeezed Pierre's hand. "Babe, I don't know what I should share and what you should hear from your mom."

"Oh, she thinks I have a mom now?"

Roz dared not state the obvious. Whether he liked it or not, yes, he had a mom alive and well and living in LA.

"I don't want to talk to whoever that is in California. I lost my mom in 2005."

Roz took a deep breath and waited. A part of her hoped he'd heard enough for one night. A shock this major should be absorbed a little at a time.

Obviously, Pierre didn't want to wait. He looked at her, his expression a mix of fear, curiosity and determination. "What did you find out that you don't want to tell me?"

Roz did not hesitate to answer him. "They have a daughter."

She felt his body stiffen beside her. "She said it happened almost as soon as she moved there, and when he found out, they got married."

Pierre emitted a laugh that contained no humor. "Now I've heard enough."

"I'm so sorry this happened, Pierre. I can't begin to imagine how you're feeling right now. Who knows how long it will take for you to get over this kind of shock, or if that's even possible. There is one more thing I feel you should know, and that is her desire to see you guys again."

Pierre's sound of disgust made it clear how he felt about that.

"She seemed to know that can only happen if you guys initiate it."

"That's not going to happen."

"I hear you, babe. I also know that how you feel later may be different than how you feel right now. So if you ever want her information…"

"I won't. You know why? Because my mother, Alana LeBlanc, the one who put my sister and me on a bus bound for Houston, left me in charge and told me she'd meet me later, survived the flood and moved across country with someone she met before the water receded. She has been living in LA since then, knowing that there were two kids believing their mom was dead."

Put that way, it sounded horrible. Roz knew she didn't have to tell that to Pierre, especially after what he said next.

"As far as I'm concerned…she still is."

Chapter 18

In the wake of Roz's atomic revelation that early Saturday morning, Pierre shut down. He locked his emotions behind a wall of indifference. Couldn't eat. Barely slept. Turned off his phone. Much like what had happened in the days and weeks after getting on a bus bound for Houston, he became quiet, distant, his cold demeanor eliciting furtive glances and whispered questions among the staff. Unlike all those years ago, he spent the few hours not working with a bottle of top-shelf vodka until reaching a stupor that not even dreams could penetrate. His body endured the abuse for less than two days. Seven hours after downing too much alcohol and too little food, he was violently awakened by his liver's demand to pay homage to the porcelain god. He heaved up his toenails, then lay on the cool marble and, with his world spinning, held on to the floor. With more precision than a bass drum in a marching band, a sledgehammer of pain beat against his temples and behind his right eye. The booze-induced vertigo jarred his senses and loosened the hold he had on his heart. The protective wall shattered. Emotions toppled out haphazardly, bumping into and rolling over each other—a rushing waterfall of anger, sadness, despair. Helpless to fight it, Pierre did something that was totally out of character. He rolled over, pulled himself into a fetal position and released more than a decade of unshed tears.

He cried himself to sleep. In the dream, urgent hands

shook his body as the sound of his name bounced off cavernous walls.

"Pierre! Pierre, wake up!"

He frowned, tried to retreat into himself, as the movements became more forceful, the voice louder.

"Pierre! Come on, brother. Wake up!"

Another second and the hands fell away, the voices stilled. Pierre relaxed, welcoming the fog of unconsciousness creeping over his—

Ice water! His body lurched forward and an anguished, distressed cry torn from his soul hurled past cotton mouth and cold, chapped lips to shatter the silence. The fog was doused by a torrent of ice-cold liquid now streaming over him and dripping from his hair.

He stumbled to his knees and locked eyes with an uninvited intruder, fearless and unapologetic, holding a now empty Waterford crystal vase.

"Lizzy? What the hell?"

"Don't you dare use that tone with me, big brother. Now that I know you're not dead I could kill you!"

She spun around and walked out of the bathroom. A somewhat disoriented Pierre followed her.

"What are you doing here?"

"What are you doing, period? Why aren't you at the restaurant? Where is your phone?"

"I turned it off."

"Why?"

"Obviously, I didn't want to talk to anyone." Pierre walked over to his nightstand and picked up a bottle of water. He opened it, took a long swig and flopped on the bed. The relentless pounding he'd felt before passing out was now a dull thud in his forehead that he tried to massage away.

Lisette watched him. An expression of concern replaced

anger as her eyes traveled from him to around a room, unusually meticulously clean, that now, like her brother, was completely disheveled and smelled like a bar. Seeing something near Pierre's feet, she walked over and slowly lifted an empty vodka bottle from beneath the bed.

"What is this doing here? You don't drink."

"I did this weekend."

She sat on the edge of the bed. "Pierre, what's wrong?"

There was a long pause before he mumbled, "Work stuff. A lot going on."

"A lot going on is nothing new. But it's never kept us from talking. I called, texted, left messages at the restaurant, even called your home phone."

"You know I never answer that thing."

"Why didn't you return my calls, especially the 9-1-1 I texted late last night?"

"Didn't see it." He looked at her, and though his heart broke from the hurt in her eyes, his placid expression remained unchanged. "Sorry."

A sudden pain rippled across his stomach. He clinched his teeth, clutched his stomach and reached for his water.

"Did you drink that whole bottle last night?"

"Most of it."

"When was the last time you ate?"

"Don't remember."

Lisette stood, disgust and irritation nudging worry away. "Drink more water. And take a shower. You stink. I'm going to get something for that hangover and will be right back."

Pierre listened as the sound of his sister's heels reverberated off the hardwood floors downstairs. He forced himself from the bed and, grabbing the water bottle, walked directly into the high-end shower that had been custom-designed to his specifications. He turned on a screen and pushed a setting preprogrammed to activate the rain forest showerhead and body jets. He sat on a stone bench, head down, as the water temperature rose slowly, along with the pressure. For the first time since Friday, he allowed in thoughts about his mother, followed by a myriad of reasons why Lisette couldn't know that she was alive. The most important one was to protect her, of course, from a woman it turned out he barely knew at fifteen, and who he certainly didn't know now.

Lisette, who with the help of continued therapy had bounced back from Alana's disappearance much faster and easier than Pierre, had gone on to thrive in Houston. She'd earned a partial scholarship to the University of Texas at Austin, making the dean's list every semester on her way to an undergrad degree in psychology. Now she was less than a year from earning a double-major graduate degree in psychology and business, and was entertaining the thought of spending a year abroad before returning to get her doctorate and realizing her dream of opening her own private practice. How would finding out about her mother affect these plans? Some things in life were simply better not known.

Pierre exited the shower, passed by the mirror and recognized parts of himself again. He pulled on jeans and a T-shirt, slipped into a pair of leather house shoes and headed downstairs. Minutes later he heard the back door open, the one that led from the house to the courtyard, behind which was the garage and guest parking.

"Pierre!"

"You don't have to yell," he said, one of the few smiles that remained within him making its way to his face. It widened when he saw his restaurant's logo on the bag she carried.

"Oh, good, you're up." Lisette set the bag on a counter.

She walked over and pulled two bowls from a cabinet and spooned hot spicy gumbo into them. She pushed one toward Pierre, who'd sat in one of the high chrome-and-leather bar chairs.

"Eat."

"Thanks." Pierre slowly reached for the spoon she handed him and began stirring the contents. "Not very hungry."

Lisette dug into her purse and pulled out a bottle. "Drink this smoothie first. It will coat your stomach and help soak up the alcohol drowning your appetite."

"How do you know so much about it?"

"I'll act like you didn't just ask that of a college student."

"Yeah, I guess you're right." He reached for the bottle, opened it and took a tentative sip. "What is this?"

Lisette nodded toward the smoothie as she blew on and then downed a spoonful of gumbo.

Pierre lifted the bottle and read its contents. "Strawberry vanilla, huh? It's good."

He drank, she ate, a weird silence stretching between them. Pierre finished the smoothie and began eating the gumbo. "Riviera fixed this," he said after a couple spoonfuls. "Almost impossible to tell the difference between his and mine."

Several more minutes went by, the silence punctuated only by the sound of silver colliding with ceramic bowls. Lisette finally pulled a napkin out of the bag and, after wiping her mouth, reached for a bottle of water. She stared at her brother while opening it, continued staring as she took a long drink.

"You ready?"

"Ready for what?"

"To talk about what's really going on."

"I told you."

"Don't do that, brother."

"What?"

A soft sigh escaped as Lisette pushed away the bowl to place crossed arms on the counter. "Out of everything I have in life, our relationship has always been my most treasured possession. No matter what's ever happened I've always known I could come to you. And I have, as you well know."

Pierre nodded, but took special interest in what was at the bottom of his gumbo.

"There's never, ever been anything we couldn't share." She reached over and placed her hands on his. The spoon fell into the bowl. He hung his head. "Pear, let's not start now."

Pierre looked up and smiled as his sister reverted to a name he hadn't heard in years, one she'd used before mastering two syllable words. Long moments passed as he wrestled within himself. One side urged him to tell her. *It's her mother, too.* The other side was determined that she'd never know, at least not until he could meet this woman otherwise known as his mother and make sure that it was okay.

Lisette came around the counter. "Just tell me," she whispered.

"I can't. And believe me, it's better that you not know."

"Are you sick? Is it something—"

"I'm fine. It's nothing to do with me."

"Really? 'Nothing to do with you' had you not returning calls, shutting off your phone, getting drunk to the point of passing out and sleeping on the floor? If you don't want to tell me, I can't force you. But please don't insult my intelligence with a lie."

When Pierre said nothing more, Lisette reached across

the counter and snatched up her purse. "You're welcome," she said, with a kiss on his temple. "I'm out."

"Lizzy."

She turned.

"It's about Mom."

"The memorial? Oh, I'm so sorry." Rushing back over, she threw her arms around him. "I didn't know that thinking about her after all these years would hit you so hard."

Pierre reached behind him and gently pulled her hands from around his neck. "This isn't about the memorial. Sit down, Lizzy."

Lisette sat, a frown on her face as she stared and waited.

There was no way to say it except to say it. So that's what Pierre did. "We don't need to have a memorial for Mom."

"Why not?"

"She's alive."

They talked for two days, with Lisette finally understanding why Pierre had chased the goose.

Chapter 19

Roz the woman was worried about the man whose mother's unbelievable story was due on her editor's desk by noon Monday, which put Rosalyn Arnaud the journalist in a sticky situation. She'd worried about Pierre all weekend, even while understanding why he didn't call. She'd stayed with him Friday night after breaking the news, and for the first time they didn't make love while sharing a bed. Later, Roz realized Pierre may have been beside her physically, but his mind had begun retreating shortly after hearing the news. That's what led to her professional dilemma, the kind that forced a revelation of what a person was made of. Drew a line in the sand—character and conscience on one side, breaking news on the other. She parked her car next to Andy's and headed into *NO Beat*, unsure where the decision she'd made would take her.

She'd barely taken two sips of coffee before her boss appeared. "There you are!"

"Good morning, Andy."

"Look at you. Rough weekend?"

"I've had better."

"Come on in and let's talk about it."

Andy stepped back so that she could enter his office, and closed the door behind them. Roz took a couple more sips of coffee, trying to decide on the best approach. In the end, she followed her mother's advice about removing gauze from a sore. *Don't be tentative, baby. Rip it off!*

"I'm going to reimburse the paper for last week's air-fare to LA. We can't run the story."

"Why not?"

"Several reasons, including the potential for a lawsuit." Pierre hadn't exactly mentioned this, but if need be Roz would make sure it came up. "The more research I did the more I've determined that the liability and potential human collateral outweigh what might be gained from breaking this story."

"Human collateral? As in someone might die? Journalists don't care about that. What matters?" He counted off on his fingers. "Is it true? Can it be verified? Will people want to read it? If it's true and can be verified, then a lawsuit can be handled. Will people want to read about someone assumed dead but found alive? Here in the city of the dead, of all places?" He smiled. "I think so."

"I respect your opinion, Andy. You haven't positioned *NO Beat* as a contender with major papers here and nationally without knowing your stuff. That fact contributed to my rough weekend." Roz chuckled, trying to lighten the moment. "But I have made the decision not to write this story. That's my gut and it's the 90 percent part. So I'll stand by it."

"I'm not happy about that, Roz."

"I understand."

"What are you working on?"

Roz shared a couple ideas.

"You need to rethink the living dead. Or come up with something as good. I'll get the receipts for the trip."

Andy's easygoing manner had been replaced by a brusque dismissal, underscored by him gathering papers on his desk and turning around to file them.

"I'll write a check as soon as I get them. On my way to follow up on a tip from last night. I'll be back around two?"

"Hopefully, with a story we can run in two days."

Roz left *NO Beat* without a destination in mind. *Home perhaps, to update my résumé?* The truth about a tip was a bit of a stretch. She had possibilities. Upcoming elections, a variety of festivals, a local designer creating fleur-de-lis-inspired fashions with metal and chains. Nothing appealed to her. No story could. Her head and heart were focused on Pierre, Lisette and Alana LeBlanc, now Lana Stern.

Roz tapped her Bluetooth to call him again. Her thumb hovered over his name, then tapped on an incoming call from a private number.

"Roz Arnaud."

"Hey, girl, it's Tiffany."

Roz had met Tiffany at her first job right out of college. They'd worked together only briefly before Tiffany moved to Atlanta, but they'd kept in touch via social media and passed on information one thought could benefit the other.

"Hi! It's been a while since I've heard from you. Are you back here?"

"No, still in Atlanta, which is why I'm calling you. How quickly can you get to Shreveport?"

"It's a five-hour drive, over three hundred miles, so unless I can get a flight—"

"Try and get a flight. After I tell you what's happening you'll want to be there."

Roz didn't even go home to pack. She went to the airport, hopped on a plane, rented a car in Shreveport, and when she returned to work on Tuesday it was with an exclusive involving a successful middle-aged businesswoman carrying a young rapper's baby, and pictures of the happy couple to prove it. Andy told her she'd pulled a rabbit from a ball cap. For now she was still on the *NO Beat* team.

After checking work emails and getting updates from her sources about a couple stories for next week, Roz was happy to call it a day. After yesterday's unexpected whirl-wind with no rest and little food, she looked forward to going home, having a simple meal delivered and finding something mindless to watch on TV.

Five minutes into her ride home, all that changed.

"Pierre, hi. I'm glad you called."

"Hey, Roz."

"How was your weekend?"

"Pretty brutal."

Roz bit her lip as her heart cracked a little bit.

"Can you come over?" Pierre asked.

"Sure. When?"

"Right now. Lizzy's here. I told her. She has questions."

"I'm on my way."

Roz made it across town in record time, pulled into one of the guest parking spaces and hurried across the courtyard. She'd wanted to meet Pierre's sister since they'd started dating. But not under these circumstances.

Pierre met her at the door and without a word pulled her into his arms. She felt his erratic heartbeat, and how it calmed as he held her and took a couple deep breaths.

"Thanks for coming," he whispered.

"Of course."

He took her hand. "Come on. Lizzy's in here."

Roz walked in, expecting to see a female version of Pierre. Instead she found a petite cocoa cutie with bright, haunting eyes, a short, naturally curly hairstyle and curves everywhere.

"Roz, this is my sister, Lisette."

Lisette stood. "Hi."

Instinctively, Roz bypassed a handshake for a hug. "I've heard so much about you," she said.

"Can I get you something to drink?"

"Actually, a cup of tea would be wonderful."

Both women watched Pierre reach for a set of keys on a silver tray.

Lisette walked over and gave him a hug, before continuing to the kitchen. "I love you, Pear."

"I love you, Lizzy."

"Heading out?" Roz asked him.

"Going to check on things at the restaurant. Haven't been in for a couple days. And even when I was there, I wasn't there. Will you stay until I get back?"

Roz nodded. "As long as you want."

She watched him leave, then turned and went to the kitchen. Lisette had found a large container with a wide selection of teas on the counter. She filled a kettle with water and headed for the cabinets.

"Can I help?"

"You can see if there is anything resembling a lemon in the fridge, but I doubt it." Lisette shook her head as she opened more cabinets. "A chef who owns a restaurant should keep food in the house."

Roz smiled. "You would think. Nope, nothing resembling a lemon, or any other type of citrus."

"I found sugar."

"That'll be fine."

The kettle whistled. Lisette poured water into two mugs. The ladies opened their tea preferences.

"How'd you meet her?"

The question, asked in a soft but determined voice, came as Roz stirred in sugar.

"From the beginning, or once I reached LA?"

"Everything. Pierre told me what happened, but I want to hear it from you."

They sat on the chairs Pierre and Lisette had used earlier to help bring him back from his drunken binge. Roz did as Lisette requested, starting with her experience of losing Aaron and the family's relief when he was found, to Alana's home in LA and the discovery that Pierre and Lisette had a sister. Lisette listened intently, asked few questions.

"For your mother to be found alive never entered my mind," Roz finished. "But once it was discovered, I had to tell Pierre and knew he would tell you."

"He didn't want to, thought it would be too devastating."

"Is it?"

"Honestly, I don't know what it is. Or how to feel. I used to dream of her coming back. I'd tell myself that she wasn't dead, make up some crazy reason she'd been delayed—kidnapped, in a coma, amnesia. But I'd daydream in class that any minute she was going to appear in the doorway, that I'd run into her outstretched arms and she'd give me the biggest hug."

Lisette's smile was bittersweet.

"Now getting that hug is possible," Roz murmured.

"And I don't know if I want it." Lisette looked contemplative as she sipped her tea. "Although I'm sure some of that is Pierre's influence. Even back then he was so angry at Mom for leaving."

"He's still angry."

"Oh, he's much angrier now. To know she's alive and knows about us and never reached out?"

"And you?"

"I'm angry, hurt. But also curious, and the more the reality of the news sinks in, grateful, even a little bit happy. But I have so many questions, even basic ones, like what is she like?"

"She's very pretty," Roz began, narrowing her eyes as she remembered the visit. "Poised. Guarded, as you might expect. Very put together."

"Wow. That does not sound like Mom at all."

Lisette asked and Roz shared everything else she could, about the house, Sherman Oaks and her glimpse of Lisette's half sister.

"I think I want to meet her," Lisette said.

"Why?"

Both women turned to see Pierre in the doorway. Neither had heard him come in.

Chapter 20

"I think that's a fair question," Roz said, breaking the silence. "Continuing to talk about and share all of what you're feeling will probably be good for both of you. Getting it all out, whether it's anger or sadness or grief…"

"She's right, brother."

"Okay, let's talk."

Roz eased off the high bar chair. "I can leave if you want."

"No." Sister and brother spoke as one.

"Okay, but can we go into the other room and get comfy?"

The three headed into a formal sitting room with an oversize couch, velvet recliner and bright yellow beanbag chair that were all decidedly informal. Lisette plopped on the beanbag, squirming around until it fitted her body. Pierre chose the couch. Roz sat there, too.

Pierre started right in. "She abandoned you, Lizzy. Why would you want to meet a woman who could do that?"

"Why not? If anything, I deserve answers to the questions I've harbored for all these years. Why she did it. How she could do it. What was her life like before then? How is it now? Who is this man she left us to marry. Who is my half sister?"

"I wonder about all of those things, too. But is learning the truth of any of it going to change what happened? No. And as far as I'm concerned there is no answer, no justification for abandoning your kids. No matter what."

"Maybe not, but I want to hear her side of it." Lisette

paused, quickly turning to Roz. "What about Grand-Mère? What happened to her?"

Pierre's intense gaze said he wanted to know that answer, too.

"She died there, at the house."

Pierre looked up. "They found her?"

"Your mother found her, but either couldn't save her or it was too late to even try, which is what she said led to the breakdown. Why she was treated for her injuries and then transferred to a mental hospital."

"I can understand that," Lisette said, slowly nodding. "Finding someone you love under those traumatic conditions could break anyone."

Pierre rested his head against the back of the couch and stared at the ceiling. "She was well enough to meet a man, move with him to LA and get married. If she could do that, she could have come back and gotten us."

Lisette rocked the beanbag into more of a chair shape. "Maybe that's what she intended. Maybe she had every intention of coming back and something happened?"

"Yes, something happened. She got pregnant and they had a child. Family complete. No need to return for the kids she left behind."

"It's totally messed up what she did," Lisette agreed. "A horrible mother, selfishly creating another life and leaving us to fend for ourselves."

Pierre nodded. "Those are the facts."

"Here we thought she was dead, and all this time she's known where we are, followed our lives via internet, while she created a different one for herself."

"Exactly."

"If she were dead, we'd never get the chance to tell her how those actions affected us. The permanent scars that those who are abandoned constantly carry. If she were dead…" Lisette's tone shifted from forceful to reflective. "We couldn't tell her anything. We'd spend our entire lives without answers, two motherless children all alone in the world."

Except for her the room was quiet, completely still.

"But she's not dead. And no matter the circumstances, we are not motherless. Yes, I am angry, hurt, disappointed, disillusioned. I will never forget what she did back then. But I can forgive her, and have some type of relationship with who she is now. In all my years of therapy, and education in psychology since then, the goal is always to heal. To be whole. That happens in different ways for different people. For me, I think reconnecting with my mom will help me continue to get better. What about you, Pierre?"

He shook his head. "I'm good."

They continued to talk. Roz had pizza delivered. Lisette decided that rather than fly back to Austin, she'd drive her rental. When Pierre resisted the idea and said she should spend the night, she assured him that the time to think and process all she'd learned would be therapeutic. Roz offered her continued support and, if needed, to be a listening ear.

"Still want me to stay?" Roz asked when Lisette was gone.

Pierre nodded, pulled her to him on the couch, but remained quiet.

"Hey, babe, while you have time with your thoughts I'll go take a shower. A last-minute assignment in Shreveport made for a late night and long day. Plus I need to call my neighbor to see if she'll feed Banner and take him for his walk. I'll see you when you come upstairs." She leaned over and gave him a gentle kiss.

He wasn't downstairs long. Roz found out when she felt his hardness press against her softness and a hand slide the loofah sponge down her back. They made love there, amid cascading water that, along with their bodies, refreshed their minds and lightened their hearts. Later, she lay with her head against his chest, wearing one of his oversize T-shirts as she idly rubbed his skin.

"I'm proud of you, Pierre," she whispered. "You and Lisette think very differently, and while speaking your opinion, you didn't try and change her mind. As hard as this is for you, there are some who would have broken under this kind of news, this much pressure. You're handling it beautifully, Pierre, showing that you are a strong, intelligent, compassionate man."

"Don't give me too much credit," he answered. He adjusted his pillow, nestled down to sleep. "Today went okay. But there's always tomorrow."

Chapter 21

Considering last week's life-changing events, Roz was thankful the remainder of this week was almost normal. The businessman/rapper article received a huge response and was picked up by the Associated Press, always a good thing. She and Pierre had been together every night, at his house or hers. Pleasurable, but exhausting. Back-to-back parties at his restaurant would keep Pierre's hands full. Roz often dreaded a weekend without plans, but she looked forward to doing this Friday what she'd planned on Tuesday before Pierre called. After a quick trip to the mall, and a stop at her favorite Italian restaurant, Roz headed home. Halfway there, her phone rang. She looked at the dash and saw a number she didn't recognize.

"Roz Arnaud."

"Hi, Roz. It's Lisette."

"Lisette, hi. How are you?"

"Okay, considering."

"I'm glad you called. What's going on?"

"It's about my grandmother, Grand-Mère Juliette. I was thinking about the person who found my mom, and was wondering if those same resources could be used to try and find my grandmother's body and give her a proper goodbye."

"I would be more than happy to ask him, and I'm sure he'd help. But we'd need something from either you or Pierre for a positive match."

"A DNA sample?"

"That's correct. It's fairly easy to get these days. I could have Flint overnight you a kit. The instructions are simple and right on the box. Then you'd overnight back the results and we'd be off to the races."

"Sure, I can do that, no problem."

"Then just text me your address and other contact information, email, phone number, and we'll get it started."

"Thanks, Roz. That means a lot."

"You're welcome."

"I'm glad you two are dating. I'm worried about Pierre."

"His reaction?"

"That, too, but especially how I found him one day passed out in the bathroom."

"Oh, no!"

"He probably wouldn't want me to tell you, okay? So you don't know. But when I arrived last Monday, that's where he was. With an empty vodka bottle beneath his bed."

"I've never seen him drink hard liquor."

"Which is probably why the night didn't go so well. But that's only part of it. I came up because days went by and I couldn't reach him. We always take each other's calls. Now, knowing why he was upset, and seeing how much animosity he still has after all these years…it scares me."

"Lisette…or should I call you Lizzy?"

"No! Sorry, but except for my brother I hate that name." Roz laughed.

"Seriously, he is the only one who can call me Lizzy and I am the only one who can call him Pear."

"How'd that nickname come about?"

"Because when I was little, I couldn't say Pierre. Pear is the closest I could get."

"It's understandable that you'd be concerned for your brother. It's been the two of you against the world practically all of your life. From the outside looking in, I might see things a bit differently."

"You're not worried?"

"I believe Pierre is a very strong man who can get through anything, even this. Have you considered all of this from his perspective? A fifteen-year-old who promised his mom he'd look after his younger sister until she arrived? Except she never did. Pierre has succeeded beyond anyone's expectations, perhaps even his own. He overcame extreme difficulties to do that. Your mother's absence was a huge part of the hardship.

"You were younger. Adjustment was easier. You remember less, didn't see or understand as much. I believe at some point Pierre will come around, and at the very least will want to meet your mom. But right now, he's working through his anger at his own pace. We should give him room and time to do that."

"I agree. Thanks, Roz."

"You're welcome."

"It was good to meet you. I'm glad you're in his life."

"Well, speaking of, he's calling now. I can call you later if you'd like."

"I'd appreciate that."

"Okay. Bye." Roz switched the call. "Hey, babe!"

"What are you doing tonight?"

"Hopefully nothing, even though I know Stefanie might be home this weekend and drag me out with her. If so, do you want us to stop by the restaurant?"

"No."

"Okay…" Her response was long and drawn out, clearly a question.

"You want to know why?"

"Sure."

"Because we're going to Texas."

"We are?"

"Yes. It's the restaurant New Orleans's twenty-fifth anniversary."

"Your mentor, Marc?"

"I got a call from a guy named Ennis, the restaurant manager, who asked if I'd come down and surprise him. Even before he finished asking I was in."

"Pierre, that's fabulous. What about your own restaurant, though?"

"That's the one good thing that came from this week's bad news. Riviera proved that he can handle the kitchen as well as me. I can expand the business, do some other things now that I know I have a solid second."

Three hours later, Roz and Pierre arrived in Houston by private plane. What the staff thought of Pierre was evident in how they treated him, starting with being picked up in a stretch limousine and put up at a five-star hotel. He and Roz stopped at the hotel only long enough to drop off their luggage and then continued to the restaurant.

"Lots of memories from this place," Pierre stated, as they pulled out of the parking lot and into Friday night traffic.

"Said with such nostalgia. Weren't you just here? Your restaurant hasn't even been open six months."

"Oh, no. It's been about two years since I worked at New Orleans. Spent a year in culinary school and almost a year in New York and back home. There was a lot of time spent behind the scenes before those doors opened in July."

"I am so impressed with everything about you. The title of your restaurant is definitely misleading."

He leaned toward her. "No, even hard is easy when it's your passion." He ran a hand down the side of her face, neck and lower, to where a hint of cleavage was exposed. "Later tonight, I'll show you exactly what I mean."

Ennis, the New Orleans restaurant manager, called and reviewed the evening's program. Roz was surprised to learn that even she would play a part in the surprise. When they arrived, Pierre was whisked in back, while she was taken into the main dining area and introduced to some of the staff, then was seated in an area reserved for friends and past employees. Marc arrived with an entourage of family and immediately became the life of the party. He had a no-nonsense way about him, with a wry sense of humor beneath the surly facade.

Several people stood and shared stories of what the New Orleans restaurant had meant in their lives. All too quickly, it was Roz's turn to go to the microphone.

"Hello, Marc. You don't know me. My name is Roz and I'm from New Orleans."

She paused as some people clapped and cheered.

"Recently, a restaurant opened that has taken the city by storm. The owner is one of your protégés." She saw Marc Fisher turn and look around the room. "As you know, Friday nights are busy. Pierre really wanted to be here, and sent this special greeting."

Everyone turned to where a white screen hung from the ceiling. A video began, of a smiling Pierre against a plain background.

"Hey, Marc. You know that there are absolutely no words to say for what you've meant in my life. Almost everything I know about what goes on in a kitchen I learned from you. Wish I could be there. Because if I were, man, I would show you how much better I prepare your specialty dish. That's right, Marc. I'd start with your signature dish, and make it better than you!"

The crowd's focus swung between the screen and Marc's antics, as he raised his fists and screamed that not even in Pierre's dreams could he come close to doing so.

"Marc, I'd serve all of those wonderful guests in your restaurant my take on *your* famous take on the Oyster Rockefeller, the Houston Oysters!"

He held up a tray of yummy-looking treats. The shot widened as Pierre began walking. Eyes were on Marc as the hallway became familiar and it suddenly dawned on him that Pierre was there! The restaurateur jumped up and ran toward the back, meeting Pierre as the door opened, and almost upending the tray. One of the assistants managed to take it away before Marc grabbed Pierre in a bear hug.

The room erupted in cheers. With tears streaming down his cheeks, and Pierre's eyes rather bright, too, Marc swung his arm around his friend's neck. That's how they entered the dining room, to sustained applause.

The assistant brought the tray Pierre had carried to Marc's table, followed by a team of waiters with trays for the room. Pierre accepted the microphone from the evening's host. Marc used a big linen napkin to unabashedly wipe his eyes.

"Ennis, I think we got him."

Ennis nodded as Pierre and the crowd laughed and applauded.

"When I heard there was a program being put together to celebrate twenty-five years of some of the best creole food outside of New Orleans, there was no way I'd miss it," Pierre went on. "For me this place, that man, changed everything. When I arrived here in Houston almost fifteen years ago, I was in the lowest place of my life. Hungry, too," he said with a laugh, "which is how I ended up here. And broke. I literally needed to work for my food.

"It would turn out to be the best meal I ever ate, one that would start me on the road to my dreams and have me standing here tonight to help honor a man who is my friend, mentor, father figure…and an alright cook. Marc Fisher."

The party went until midnight, with Marc entertaining his table by regaling them with stories of Pierre's teenaged years. Roz had never seen Pierre this happy, and she herself hadn't laughed so hard in a very long time. With promises to see each other soon for more quality time, the crowd eventually dispersed and headed to their cars.

In the limo, Roz leaned her head against Pierre's shoulder. "You know what I thought tonight, as you gave your speech?"

"Hmm?"

"I thought about life's ironies and how we can never predict the outcome. I know you hate your mom, but in a weird, twisted way, her abandoning you and Lisette brought you here. It sucked at the time, but had she come back to get you, who knows what would have happened?"

Pierre shrugged. "I don't know."

"But we know what happened because you stayed. Just an interesting way to look at things."

He raised a brow. "Didn't you mention talking to Lisette today?"

"Yes, and no, this perspective isn't a result of talking with her. In fact, when it came to how you feel about your mom and whether or not you should meet her, I told her that it was your right to be as angry as you wanted for as long as you needed. That each of you has different memories from different experiences, so how you interact with your mom, or not, may end up being totally different, too."

"You told her that?"

"I did."

"Thank you, baby. You're smarter than you look."

Roz punched him. Pierre wrapped his arms around her to stop the assault. The ride became quiet, as she took in Houston's downtown skyline and imagined a young Pierre trying to survive in the sprawling city. Once inside the hotel suite, the lovers made love as they took a shower, then crawled into bed and did it again. Their flight back to New Orleans was not until noon. With her body fully sated, Roz relaxed, closed her eyes and welcomed blissful sleep.

"What would I say to her?"

Roz's eyelids fluttered. Was she dreaming or was that Pierre? She shifted to face him. "What, babe?"

"If I saw my mother again, what would I say?"

Roz pondered his question. "Maybe start with hello?"

"That's a given. I'm talking about after the superficial pseudo-sociable how-are-you-doing bull crap. I'm older now, but when I think of her it's with the emotions of right after I last saw her. It's the fifteen-year-old Pierre. That kid was so angry. Blamed her for everything. What she did was wrong and I don't know how trying to say that to her face would go."

"There's no way we can ever know what will happen in any given situation. But I know what will happen if you don't meet her. Nothing. And maybe that's okay. It's for you to decide. But while you're deciding, think of that fifteen-year-old who blamed her for everything. Because part of that everything is the amazing man you are today."

Chapter 22

Another week went by. Roz and Pierre continued to grow closer. The light, easygoing mood of the man she'd met returned. Roz would like to think she was part of the reason. But a second reason had to be the invitation he'd gotten to join another popular Chow Channel star on a segment being filmed in Europe. Pierre had received the text yesterday morning, would board a plane for London late this afternoon, shoot for two days, and return to the States either Thursday or Friday. Roz was tempted to go, but he discouraged it, only because he knew they'd be working almost nonstop. He suggested the two of them fly over after the holidays, when after the kind of rush Easy Creole Cuisine anticipated, he'd be more than ready for a vacation.

Roz had observed something else. With each passing day since their trip to Houston, Pierre moved ever so slightly closer to the possibility of someday considering a conversation with his mom. Lisette was sure that she wanted to talk with her but at her therapist's suggestion promised to consider waiting until after getting her master's degree. While she felt ready, the truth was there was no way to really know what impact seeing her mother would have on her, what hidden emotions, feelings or memories would come up. The year she planned to take off before going for her doctorate would be a good time to bring the past and the present back together.

Work was back on track for Roz. After using freelancers for the past three months, Andy had finally hired Ginny's permanent replacement. Paige was a native to the city with connections everywhere, resulting in the gossipy-style stories the editor-in-chief and the public craved. Those two had their heads together from Paige's first day. Roz felt it might not be long before other body parts came together, as well. Fine by her. They were both single and both adults. Roz had more time to develop relevant, news-oriented stories, and with the holidays approaching there'd be no lack of social, civic and business topics that, with a unique perspective or spin, could make for great reading.

Roz pulled out her laptop and was double-checking her research when her cell phone face lit up. She tapped the screen and saw a missed call from Flint. She opened her desk drawer, put on her headset and returned the call.

"Good morning, Flint. You must have phoned just as I went to get coffee. What's going on?"

"I'm following up with that last case you gave me. Juliette LeBlanc?"

"Right."

"And the DNA sample from her granddaughter, Lisette?"

"Did you find a match?"

"I did. I found her."

"That's excellent, Flint. Lisette will be so happy to hear that news. Can you send over all the particulars, the claim forms and—"

"I'm ahead of you, Roz. Putting together an email with all of that. You'll get it in a few."

"You're the man."

"I try."

"Thanks. Talk to you later."

"Oh, Roz."

"Yes."

"Regarding that info on the other case you needed. Did you get it?"

"What other case?"

"The other LeBlanc. The one in California."

A slow chill began at the nape of her neck and slid down her spine. "I didn't request a resend, Flint."

"Not directly. But somebody called and had it sent over to you."

Roz pulled her laptop closer, began typing notes. "What day was this?"

"Early last week. Monday or Tuesday. The call came in to the office phone, so I don't have a time stamp right in front of me."

"I didn't request that."

"Sorry, Roz. It sounded legit."

"No worries. It's probably a mix-up on this end. Take care."

Roz hung up the phone as Andy's door opened. Paige threw back her hair, tossed a flirty look over her shoulder and closed the door. Her eyes widened when she saw Roz, who rarely came in before nine or nine thirty.

"Oh! Hi, Roz."

"Good morning."

Roz noted her jumpy reaction as she passed her on the way to Andy's office. She tapped the door lightly and then opened it. "Got a minute?"

"Roz! You're here early."

Was she imagining things or was that a shade of light red creeping up his neck?

"We've got a problem."

"We do?" Andy leaned back in his chair, laced his fingers together behind his head.

"Playing stupid doesn't become you, Andy."

"How am I supposed to know what you're talking about?"

"Who called Flint from this office?"

"Oh, that." He gave a little smile and didn't meet her eyes.

Roz walked over and sat in a chair in front of his desk. "Why?"

"It's not personal, Roz. It's business. You're not the only one who has connections."

"Oh, really. So that's why you called my connection, used my name and finagled information out of him?"

"It's a small world, Roz. You're not the only person who knows Flint."

"Yes, but I'm the only one who had the name you, or someone you put up to it, extracted private information about."

"I was curious. As journalists, we're cutthroat. We get the story. You got it and then squashed it. Made me more and more determined to solve the mystery. Who would Roz hold back a story for, one that could be nationally recognized? Then I found out. Pierre LeBlanc. Wow. Lost his mom, or so he thought. Life goes on and then out of the blue, she reappears. How did you get the lead on that?"

Roz's stomach knotted and roiled. "Don't run the story, Andy."

"Not your story anymore, Roz. Paige stumbled on a real breaker."

Roz got the whole picture with that one line. "Have you interviewed her? The mom?"

"This past weekend. Saturday and Sunday. Good human interest angle. Mother missing her kids. Wants to get back in their lives but doesn't know how. Public appeal. A family reunited. The city will eat it up and love LeBlanc even more."

"So you've talked to Pierre?"

"No, we figured that's what you tried and that's what brought you into my office refusing to release his name."

"Then how can you possibly imagine this having a happy ending?"

"We can hope. But how it ends isn't the main focus.

Generating the buzz is what we're after. And we don't need an interview with the chef for that."

"You're a great journalist, Andy, and a good person with a conscience, and integrity. Or so I thought. This news has devastated Pierre and his sister who are trying to regain their life's equilibrium after having their world rocked. A hard enough job handled privately. The news going public could destroy lives, careers. I'm asking you as a colleague and a friend. Don't do this."

Andy cocked his head. "Are you sleeping with him?"

Roz leaped over the desk, punched the editor in the chest and then slapped him senseless. In her mind.

"Are you sleeping with Paige?" she countered instead, and stood. "So after a year and a half, this is where we're at, you and I?"

"It's not our first difference of opinion, Roz."

"But it's a deal breaker, Andy. Look, let's figure out how we can both feel comfortable with this. I'll do the story. I'll interview Pierre and his sister. Do a follow-up call with the mom. But if you want a well-rounded, unbiased article, and that's the type we should run with a topic like this, then it's only fair that all parties know what's coming out in the paper before the first customer who buys it off the street."

"You can give Pierre and whoever else a heads-up if you'd like. Tell them the story is running tomorrow."

"Oh, so I was also going to be in the dark. You and Paige have obviously worked on this from the time she was hired." Roz looked at Andy, but instead of him, she saw a job she loved and that she'd worked at over a year and a half begin to fade away. If the story ran, she'd quit. There was no way she'd work for someone who'd betray her.

"Should I clean out my desk now?"

"Come on, Roz. You're being overly dramatic about

something that hasn't even happened yet. This might turn out better than any of us could imagine. Read the article. Wait and see the chef's response. The city's response. All of this may be much ado about nothing."

"I surely hope so, Andy. Meanwhile I need to step out of the office and make some calls."

Roz dared not look at Paige, the young woman who'd given her a sugary greeting while hiding a bloodstained knife. She gathered up her purse and laptop, her fingers already tapping Pierre's number before she was out of the door.

The call went to voice mail. "Pierre, hi, it's me. I know you're eight or nine hours ahead over there, so whenever you get this message, please give me a call. It's important that I talk with you as soon as possible. Okay? Hope all is going well." Roz paused, almost added, "I love you."

But instead, she said goodbye, scrolled to Lisette's name and placed the call.

Chapter 23

"Roz? Hello? Roz… I can't hear you. Wait. Let me walk around a bit."

"Cell phone's almost impossible here, mate."

Pierre nodded at the cameraman who'd stated the obvious. He sent a quick text instead and within minutes was called back onto the set, on a private island owned by the show's producer. The scenery was idyllic. The castle, with its three-story ceilings, countless bedrooms and baths, three custom kitchens and a working moat, was something out of another era. For Pierre, so was their cell reception.

Because of Wednesday's intense filming schedule, cast and crew spent Tuesday night in the castle. Before going to bed he was given the use of a satellite phone and again tried reaching Roz. The call went to voice mail. Filming wrapped up late Wednesday night. The group of almost thirty people boarded a yacht back to London. As the city lights came into view cell phone service kicked in, evidenced by Pierre's message and missed call indicators pinging for what felt like five minutes straight. Thinking it might have something to do with Lisette, he jerked the phone out of its holder and began to scroll. There were a ton of texts and messages from Cathy, Don, Ed, Riviera, Lisette, friends from around the country, Roz—many times—and a slew of media and entertainment television outlets.

Remembering Roz's message from yesterday, and bursting with news to share with her today, he clicked on the text icon, found hers and scrolled up.

Pierre, that was a really bad connection. Assuming we got disconnected. Very important that I talk with you soonest. Please call back.

The next one, sent an hour later.

Babe, just tried calling again. Sending this text because of time-sensitive news. Don't want to upset you but it's urgent. Call tonight, no matter what time, before news breaks tomorrow.

Pierre's brow creased as he scrolled to the next message, this one with a link attached. It was sent Wednesday morning, at four forty-two.

I hate sharing this by text but have found no way to reach you and you need to know ASAP. No easy way to say this either. The story about your mom being alive is in today's edition of NO Beat.

What? He sat up, wiped his eyes. It had been a couple of nonstop days and nights for him and the crew. He was a little groggy. Had to be. It was the only way he could have seen what he thought he saw. He took a breath and looked again. The words were the same. *Need to know ASAP. No easy way to say this.* He finished the text.

Tried to get story pulled. Or delayed. Didn't want this. So sorry, Pierre. I am hoping for the best.

The best? What good could come out of her putting his past and what happened with his mother on display for the world to read about? Tried to get it pulled or delayed? How about not writing it in the first place? How about that?

Sitting back, Pierre found images of the past few months and their whirlwind time together playing as a video in his mind. Every act she'd done, every word, took on new meaning. All the times she'd asked about his family, and their experience during Hurricane Katrina. Was it all part of a grand plan to get the scoop on the Quarter's newest chef?

After more than a decade of Lisette being the only female he trusted, he'd opened up to Roz and shared parts of himself few others had seen, if anyone. And how had she repaid this trust? By writing an article about news so shocking he'd yet to fully process it, and printing it for anyone with an internet connection to read. Done so without even bothering to ask if telling his story was okay. *Because she knew it wasn't, and never would be. Did that matter? No!* She'd taken a private story, his story, and used it to raise her profile. She'd exploited him for his celebrity, planned to capitalize on his fame.

Pierre slumped against the chair, numb with the myriad of emotions flooding his soul. Anger. Hurt. Disappointment. Disillusion. The usual suspects. But there was one that surprised him. Loneliness. A loner by nature, he'd long felt comfortable with and had even preferred his own company. Kept his own counsel. Sharing with Roz was a new experience for him, because not only was she a friend, or so he'd thought, but his lover. Soul mate, even. A woman who'd made him think about the rest of his life, and her being in it. Rosalyn Arnaud. His Roz. The woman who seemed to understand the pain of losing someone, of having a person ripped from your life in an instant. And not only to understand, but to care.

His movements mechanical, Pierre slowly scrolled through the rest of the messages. He responded to Cathy. Yes, prepare a statement. To his handlers at Chow Channel and Intense Energy. Yes, it's true. No, I didn't authorize it. Publicist will be in touch. To Riviera. Thanks for your concern, and for taking over at the restaurant. Shocked, processing, but will get through it. He also passed on a message for the restaurant manager, Ed. To Buddha. Of all people, you can best imagine how I'm feeling right now. Will call when stateside. After sending messages to his personal manager and attorney, he revisited the message from Roz and clicked on the link. Didn't get past the first paragraph. Couldn't. An article that began by portraying his mother as a victim couldn't end well for him. Especially one written by a woman who'd acted as though she were on his and Lisette's side but had spun this story. What had happened to the straight shooter he'd fallen in love with at the Bayou Ball?

Wait...what?

There was no denying it. He loved her, and from that night. Pierre slid the phone into his shirt pocket and walked out to the yacht's stern, the only other spot on the luxurious vessel where no one was smiling, laughing and offering champagne for the success of their shoot. Before boarding the yacht, Pierre had felt like celebrating. Now? Not so much. He'd received a one-two punch that would have felled a weaker man. A story, now public, of a woman who had betrayed him way back when, written by one who'd deceived him now.

He hadn't wanted to deal with airports and crowds. His personal manager arranged a charter flight. On the way home Pierre spoke with his publicist, sous chef and business partners, but mostly with Lisette. Her phone had begun ringing within hours of *NO Beat* going on sale. Copies were being circulated around the campus. Most people were curious and understanding, but she'd begun to feel the pressure of being in the public eye and had gotten a hotel room. She shared that Roz had found their grandmother's remains, but he was so consumed with Roz's betrayal that the news barely registered. He'd hung up, braced himself and finally read the article. While he and his sister were mentioned, the story was all about Alana. The way it had been for years, Pierre thought. She'd stayed consistent, and continued being the selfish person who left her children but saved herself. There was one person he didn't call. Roz.

Pierre went straight to his restaurant. Rode his motorcycle and entered through a back door. Riviera was the first to see him.

"Chef. Didn't expect to see you here."

"I've got a business to run. Where else would I be?"

He walked into the kitchen with an authority that came naturally, but a bravado he didn't feel. When he spoke, however, he pulled off the act.

"Hey, everybody. Pull your food off the fire. Come around."

The staff quickly complied.

"Listen up because I'm only going to say this once. It's about the story in *NO Beat*. What's true is that my mom abandoned my sister and I when I was fifteen, and that she has resurfaced. Why, I don't know. I've not talked to her. And I don't want to talk about her. So here at Easy Creole Cuisine it's business as usual. *Comprende?*"

Riviera smiled, held up his hand for a fist bump. "Heard, Chef. Don't worry. We've got your back."

For the next two days, Easy Creole Cuisine wasn't easy for the workforce. The restaurant had been slammed almost from the beginning, but the increased interest in an already popular celebrity chef only added to the pressure. It didn't help that Pierre had been spotted leaving Thursday night, and his secret side entrance exposed. He arrived Friday to a horde of reporters at that door, even though he'd purposely come early. He'd smiled, pushed his way through that nightmare, then put Buddha on private body-guard duty to ensure he wouldn't get mobbed like that again. He left the restaurant that night without incident, said goodbye to Buddha at the door. It wasn't until twenty-five minutes later that he realized the bodyguard should have followed him home.

He pulled the motorcycle into its garage space, kicked down the stand and hung his helmet on the bars. Long strides made short work of the distance between him and the enemy. Roz, camping out in his courtyard. How dare she?

"What do you want?"

There was a shocked pause as the enemy absorbed the curt question. "What kind of question is that? I've called, texted, emailed and been worried sick. You've been back for two days." He watched eyes filled with fake concern search his face. "I don't blame you for being upset, Pierre, but if you read any of my messages, you'd know this was out of my control."

"Which part? Writing the story, telling your boss about it or having it published?"

"That's just it. I didn't write—"

"Stop! Don't even go there, Roz, and try and deny it. The story was published in *NO Beat*. You're the only one at that paper who knew about my mom. You dragged the details out of me, went looking for her when nobody asked you to, believed every lame excuse she offered for leaving, and then without caring how I felt about it, put all of that bullshit in the paper for everyone to see!"

"Pierre, I—"

"Why'd you do it, Roz? Knowing my history with women who've lied to me, how could you betray me? Did you do it for money? Is my mom's husband rich or famous? Did you do it for the paper, for your career, as a come up?

Or were you seeking your own fifteen minutes of fame, found out that it wasn't bright enough sharing my spotlight and went in search of your own?"

"What you're assuming is not what happened."

"Oh, really."

"If we could just go inside, sit down and—"

Pierre made the harsh sound of a buzzer. "Wrong answer, traitor. Your welcome mat's been pulled. Your number will be deleted. I'd advise you to lose mine, too, because anything you had to say to me should have happened in a conversation before you deceived me."

After searing her with a look that dared her to follow, Pierre stormed into his house and shut the door. Before she could talk him out of his anger. Before those doe-like eyes could convince him that she really was sorry, that somehow a major mistake had been made, one that would absolve her of the culpability in making his private life public and shattering his heart.

Chapter 24

Heading into the office on Monday morning, Roz was only slightly less dazed than when she'd been verbally butchered by Chef Pierre. Obviously, he'd not read her later emails, especially the one that clarified Paige as the story's author in case he'd passed over the byline. That fact even though there were others that placed Roz Arnaud right in the crosshairs, namely the one where had she not mentioned anything to Andy—nada until all her research was done, including running everything by Pierre to know how he felt about it—meant she shouldn't be a suddenly single journalist on her way to resign from the job.

She pulled into *NO Beat*'s parking lot. Her phone rang. She squelched the desire/hope/prayer/fantasy that it was Pierre.

"Hey, Stefanie."

"What? No Biff?"

"I saw Pierre."

"Uh-oh. Didn't go well?"

"Major understatement. But I can't talk now. Just pulled into *NO Beat*."

"Okay. Call me when you get off work."

"That'll be in about an hour. I'm resigning." Even the silence was silent. "A lot happened while you and your fiancé frolicked in sand on the beach."

"Phone me back as soon as you can."

The call gave Roz strength that was sorely needed. She wouldn't have a job after this impromptu meeting, but she had a best friend to call back. Once in the building she headed directly for the office at the end of the hall. That Paige was in there was no surprise. Roz had ignored her since the story broke and had no plans to change that position.

"Excuse me, Andy, do you have a minute?"

"Later, Roz. Paige and I are discussing—"

"Actually, Andy, there's a phone call that I need to return. Can I send what I have so far and discuss further after you've read it?"

"Sure."

Paige offered a hesitant smile. "Morning, Roz."

There was no hesitation in Roz's reply, directed at Andy. "This won't take long."

The door had barely closed before Roz pulled a single sheet of paper from her tote and placed it on Andy's desk.

Andy reached for it. "What's this?"

"My resignation, effective immediately."

"Ah, come on, Roz. Sit down. Let's talk this out."

"I'll have a seat but there's no changing my mind. Some ethical boundaries have been crossed that are beyond what I find acceptable. Printing a story I initiated but pulled on moralistic grounds was your prerogative. Leaving your company is mine."

"Morals? You sure you want to go there?"

"I already did, which is why this is my last day."

"You know how small our world is, Roz. Did you really think you could date the city's golden boy and have no one find out?"

A surprising revelation for sure, but Roz kept her poise.

"Given that I accompanied him to his mentor's much-publicized anniversary, I was obviously not hiding."

"You were obviously not thinking rationally either. Had that story been about anyone besides a guy you were screwing—"

"Excuse me?"

"—you would have typed up a story twice as long as the one published and demanded a banner covering the top of the page."

Roz had stood as he talked and now headed to the door. She had to—couldn't guarantee her continued professionalism otherwise.

"Roz, wait." Andy stood and headed toward her. "I didn't meant that!"

Maybe not, but Roz meant what was written on that paper. Her head remained high as she walked out the door, dialing Stefanie as she crossed to her car.

"Wow, that was fast" was Stefanie's greeting.

"Leaving kept me from going to jail."

Roz shared what had happened on the way to Gee's, then imagined Andy's face on the punching bag as she put her body through a rigorous workout. Back at the bungalow she took a long hot shower and washed her hair. Her mother called. Roz told her what had happened at work and received the kind of support and encouragement that only a mom could provide. The conversation buoyed her spirits enough for her to fire up the laptop, update her résumé and send out a few. Unable to decide on which snack food would make her feel better, she sat down with a bowl of popcorn, M&Ms and peanuts combined, found a marathon of *Friends* and tried to borrow their feel-good. Two hours later, with Mom's reassurance fading and her spirits continuing to spiral down, Roz remembered another cure for the doldrums that had never failed her. She jumped from the couch, grabbed her purse and hoped their track record would hold.

Pierre vowed to forget her. Put Roz in the past with other disappointments and people who'd failed him. People like Alana LeBlanc, now Lana Stern. The nonstop pace of the busy weekend had helped with that. But London had been Chow Channel's year-end taping and due to his increased popularity—Roz's antics notwithstanding—his people were renegotiating his contract with Intense Energy. So now he sat with the last thing he needed, time on his hands. Reaching for his phone, he scrolled the contacts for who he could call. In the months with the new business and Roz, he'd gone AWOL on business partners and silent on the few individuals who counted as friends. He couldn't feel bad when his attempts were met with two assistants, three voice mails and one full mailbox. *What about a night in New York?* One thing he loved about the city that never slept was that a perfectly good time could be had alone. He began a search on the internet for Broadway shows that ran on Monday. But his heart wasn't in it. He thought about his friend's jazz club, but just as quickly dismissed that idea. The last time he'd gone there, Roz had been with him. Her scent probably still covered the city.

The phone rang in his hand, an unexpected sound that gratefully jolted him out of memories of the woman who'd felt so good in his arms. The number on his screen had a New Orleans area code, but it wasn't a number he recognized. No way would he risk a reporter's call. Tossing his phone down, he walked to the fully stocked bar that anchored the game room. Remembering the goose that had cooked him instead of the other way around, he quickly bypassed the bottles and opened the fridge. A variety of beers lined the shelves. He picked one that was alcohol free, popped the top and took a swig. Checking out a room he rarely entered, he brushed his hand over a blackjack and poker table on his way to a contemporary pool table made of stainless steel. He picked up a stick, lined it up with the cue ball and was interrupted by the phone again, his message indicator. Curious as to which media outlet had left a voice mail, he palmed the phone with one hand and hit the speaker button to hear who'd called.

"This message is for that man who fancies himself a cook, and thinks he knows a thing or two about crawfish."

Pierre almost dropped his cell. He wasn't sure what shocked him more, that Ma had challenged his cooking skills or that she'd called him in the first place. He started to return the call, and then got a better idea.

"Ma, tell me you didn't call him just now." Roz had just spent almost thirty minutes on the hallowed ground of Ma's kitchen, sharing what had happened with her and Pierre.

"I didn't call him just now." Ma didn't wilt under Roz's intense gaze, but the astute journalist still didn't believe her.

"I called him *again* just now. I read the article, baby."

"Why didn't you tell me?"

"I did, first chance I got." Ma's smile, filled with compassion and understanding, was as warm as a hug. "Felt like you needed an ear more than a mouth when you first got here. Anyway, I read it and called him before I put down the paper. My heart goes out to that young man."

"How'd you have his number?"

"You don't have to be a journalist to get information." Ma's gray eyes twinkled, taking years off her face. "Women are born with the ability to investigate. I called the restaurant. Got a nice young man, a Mexican fellow—"

"Riviera."

Ma nodded as she headed out of the kitchen, Roz right behind. "—and told him who I was and why I was calling. He gave me the number. I called it. You being here reminded me that Pierre didn't answer and never called back. So I called him again."

Ma reached for dirty dishes on a recently vacated table.

Roz snatched up empty glasses and followed Ma into the kitchen. "Why would you do that when I'm here, after what I told you?"

"I have my reasons." Ma deposited plates in a soapy sink and crossed to the stove.

Roz didn't ask what those were. In her mind, none were good enough to invite another showdown. She crossed the small room and gave the woman a hug.

"I know you meant well, but I'm leaving."

"Suit yourself. But in five minutes I'll be ready to dish up praline cream."

Roz's favorite dessert in the world. Her mouth watered as she suppressed a groan. "You play dirty, Ma."

"Look, baby. Pierre didn't answer, so I left a message. He hasn't been back here since that last time with you, so there is little chance he'll come tonight. And if he does, he'll surely call first. So why don't you go wash your hands and try to relax while I fix your treat."

Roz did as Ma suggested and tried to relax. But she couldn't. Thoughts of her early-morning encounter with Pierre were as upsetting now as when the event had actually occurred. She wanted to enjoy the dessert, but doubted she could get it past the lump in her throat.

"Never mind about that cream, Ma. I think I'd better go." Roz reached for her tote stashed under the table.

"Too late." Ma walked toward her with a bowl of heaven. "You can't turn me down once the food's dished up."

Roz pursed her lips and tried to maintain a frown, even as the smell of toasted pecans and warm caramel drizzle tickled her taste buds and forced up the corners of her mouth. She accepted the spoon Ma held, dug through layers of cookie crust, maple filling, pecan caramel crumble and homemade vanilla ice cream. "I'll say it again, Ma," Roz began, eyes closed as she savored the flavors. "You do not play fair."

"Like my mama always said. You can catch more people with sugar than vinegar."

"More like hold them hostage, unable to leave your place until the last bite is gone."

Ma chuckled, headed toward the door to welcome two new customers. Roz got lost in the sinful sweet treat, with thoughts of Friday's confrontation and today's resignation taking a back seat to the decadent, gooey goodness in front of her.

Casual conversation with a diner she'd seen there several times before further lightened the mood as they shared memories of their first experience at the house on Carrollton. Ma had Roz at "red crawfish bucket." The diner, Lamar, who'd known "the food lady" since he was ten, shared that the first meal he'd ordered, the Old Glory Plate, was still his favorite. Roz readily admitted that she, too, loved that meal. The combination of spicy red beans and long-grain white rice topped with golden-fried nuggets of blue catfish was Ma's first signature dish and remained the most popular.

Listening to Lamar's sometimes comical, sometimes frightening memories of growing up a few doors down from a community treasure was quite entertaining. By the time Roz scraped up the last spoonful of gooey goodness, thoughts of Pierre had all but disappeared. She finished the dish, placed twice as much cash on the table as her bill demanded, and thinking to go shopping before heading home, went to freshen up.

"Well, now! Whatcha' got cookin', good-lookin'?"

Roz smiled at Ma's clever greeting, closing and locking the red wooden door. She used the facilities, reapplied gloss, then continued eyeing herself in the mirror as she fooled with her hair and thought about chopping it all off—the same as her attempts to emotionally cut Pierre from her heart. The idea was either harebrained or genius. Roz went in search of Ma to tell her which one.

"Hey, Ma. What do you think about…" Words sputtered and died out like a windblown candle. A tall, well-defined body stood at the kitchen entrance. Long, strong legs and broad shoulders she saw stiffen at the sound of her voice. Ma's jauntily delivered hello from moments before took on new meaning. Pierre LeBlanc had dangerously good looks, with skills to serve up mouthwatering masterpieces in the kitchen, and bedroom, too. Her hold on the strap of her tote tightened as she tiptoed down the short hallway and hurried toward the exit.

"Rosalyn!"

Act as though you don't hear her. She'll never know. Two more steps and she could reach for the doorknob.

"Hey, Roz. Ma's calling you."

Roz bit back an expletive, now regretting the fun conversation she'd shared with Lamar, and that she'd told him her name. She turned with the hope that Ma would come out of the kitchen. Ma did not. Roz recrossed the dining area, avoiding Pierre's disdainful stare. Ignoring the wide girth he gave her as though she was poison.

"Yes, Ma?"

"I know you weren't going to try and sneak out of my place without saying goodbye."

"It wasn't that. I just realized the time and was rushing out—"

"No, I'll leave."

Ma rose to her full height of four-eleven to block the six-foot-plus man's path. "You can if you want. But invitations to my kitchen don't come often. And I asked you here to share more than recipes."

"Yeah, I'm now fairly certain why you called."

"I didn't ask her to." Roz knew she sounded defensive. When protecting oneself, it came with the territory.

"And I didn't ask *you*," Pierre snarled, then shifted his stance to give Roz his back. "Look, Ma, I appreciate you inviting me down, I really do. But I can't stay, not as long as she's here."

"You don't have to worry about that, son," Ma answered, her voice low as she looked beyond Pierre's left arm. "She was on the way out before you got here."

Chapter 25

Pierre took a deep breath to calm himself, even as he acknowledged that he wasn't totally crazy. One question had been answered, at least. When he reached the entrance to Ma's kitchen he hadn't been hallucinating. Along with the classic aromas of Creole cuisine...he'd smelled her. The scent that he'd drowned in on so many nights, that he'd lapped up like nectar, along with the honeydew drops from her heat. Citrus and jasmine, cinnamon and sex, those nights he'd hoped would go on forever. The nights when he first began to believe that all women weren't like his mother, that there may be someone who wouldn't leave him like she did.

"She didn't write that story."

The simple act of raising his head was almost too much. "Is that what this invitation is about? You trying to defend what can't be defended?"

"No, not only that, although considering what I witnessed happening between the two of you that first night you came here, I believe she's at least worth being heard out. Tonight is about food. I've decided to do something that I haven't done in the forty-plus years I've sold affordable meals to the hungry—in this house and around the city. I'm going to pass the torch, share the secrets of the food that keeps people coming back."

Pierre's eyes became misty as her generous words reached his ears. "But...why? And why me?"

"Because you're the son I never had, for one reason. But

there's another one, too." Ma's eyes traveled from Pierre's questioning face to the clock on the wall. "Let me turn on the blue light and finish up these last customers."

Pierre watched Ma walk out of the kitchen, amazed that someone who'd met him only twice could convey more love to him in five minutes than his mother had in almost fifteen years. At the very least Ma deserved to say her piece and have him listen. The laughter that drifted in from the modest dining area was proof of how good her food made people feel. He knew how it made him feel. At the end of the day, wasn't that what cooking was all about? The experience that one's food evoked? The memories? The love?

Pierre was a bit shocked to realize that in the whirlwind of the past two years—the Chow Channel, Intense Energy, his own restaurant, Easy Creole Cuisine—the reason he'd fallen in love with cooking in the first place had been partly forgotten.

He looked around Ma's unassuming kitchen. Saw it with new eyes. The stove, sparkling white at one time, he assumed, now yellowed and encrusted, holding the burns and scorches of a thousand dances with cast-iron skillets and pots, like the one bubbling now on the right side back burner, holding what Pierre no doubt knew would make a couple sell their first child. To the right of the stove, a variety of worn, scratched cookware hung from a rusting steel holder leveled to be within Ma's easy reach. On the wall to the left were makeshift shelves of unpainted pinewood with dried herb and spice-filled containers of every shape and size filling each row. A stainless steel mobile counter took up the rest of the wall. It had seen better days, as had the wall behind it with its stained and peeling wallpaper and rotting baseboards. In that moment the reason hit Pierre like a fist. Katrina had been here and left a calling card.

Beneath the counter were what Pierre imagined to be twenty-five to fifty pound plastic bins filled with white rice and dried red beans, and shelves of smaller containers holding flour, meal, sugar and other staples. Behind him, a rickety refrigerator appeared to be a match to the stove, along with an upright, side-by-side freezer no doubt filled with locally sourced seafood and Ma's original boudin. It was a room full of misfits, rejects and make-do magic all being used to save people's lives.

Pierre heard Ma's sure footsteps and turned as she entered the kitchen. "What's the blue light?"

"Means I'm done for the night. Wanted to use a red one to indicate I'd stopped serving, but people might have mistaken that to mean I was serving up something else!"

Pierre laughed at Ma's boldness, an easy mirth that continued for the next hour as they cooked side by side. Ma wouldn't let him write down the secrets she shared, but provided tips to help him remember.

"Holy trinity, divinity, spice. All call, black ball, always nice."

A catchy saying that translated into the ingredients for Ma's original spice mix. Pierre eyed her movements like a hawk, soaked up the knowledge like a sponge. After setting a mix of her signature spicy sausage to marinate, Ma poured two glasses of sweet tea, gave them to Pierre and ordered him out of the kitchen. She came behind him moments later with two steaming bowls of jambalaya. Now that Pierre had peered behind the magic, the food seemed even more delicious.

He ate several spoonfuls, then set down the spoon and wiped his mouth. "I still can't believe you did what you did."

"Shared my secrets?" Ma shrugged. "Wouldn't have done the world much good to take them to the grave."

Pierre nodded. Since finding out about Alana he'd become more aware of life and death conversations, and they'd taken on new meaning. Recent events with his mother and Roz had further ground home the point that one could be alive but dead inside, and dead but really alive. Pierre was living, breathing, moving, functioning. But without Roz in his life… It was a thought he forced his mind not to finish. To do so would be an acknowledgment that he missed her. He couldn't do that.

He could get another question answered, though, one that had bugged him all evening. He leaned against the plastic chair, rocked it off the floor. "Earlier you said that sharing spice secrets was only one of the reasons you invited me here. Was Roz the other?"

"Yes and no."

"I don't understand that answer."

"I know, but you will." Ma pushed the half-eaten bowl of jambalaya away from her and took a long drink of tea. After wiping her mouth with a napkin, she folded her hands before her and peered into Pierre's eyes.

"I knew your mama."

Pierre didn't say a word for forty-five minutes. When he left, even before driving away from the curb in front of Ma's he dialed Roz's number. The call went to voice mail.

He grappled with whether or not to leave a message and decided against it. If Roz didn't answer because she was angry with him, leaving a message wouldn't matter. If she didn't want to see him again didn't matter either. They would have at least one more face-to-face conversation. That much was up to Pierre. What happened after he said what he said would be up to Roz.

"Is that him?"

It was just past eleven. After an evening of going crazy

inside her head and swearing that she wouldn't bring Stefanie into her drama, Roz was on the phone with her BFF.

"Well, is it?" Stefanie repeated, an octave higher than before.

"Yes, but I'm not answering it."

"Why not? We can talk later. You and Pierre need to talk now."

"Have you forgotten what I just told you about earlier tonight? Pierre is still very angry with me and I don't blame him. Trust me when I tell you that he and I don't even need to see each other, let alone have a conversation."

"He called, Roz. One only does that when they want to communicate with who's on the other end of the line."

"Communicate or curse out."

"It's talking either way."

"I don't need any more of that type of talk. I already feel bad enough."

"That's because you insist that this is all your fault, Roz, but it's not. You didn't write the article and you didn't tell Andy about Pierre."

"True, but had I not said anything at all—hadn't mentioned the subject to Andy, even generally, hadn't flown to LA on company time or used their funds, there wouldn't have been a story. When it comes to breaking news, Andy's a bloodhound. I should have known that after telling him and then tabling the subject would only ratchet up his curiosity. Should have anticipated he'd go around me to gain information. Should have driven home the point to Flint that what he'd shared with me had to remain confidential. But I didn't do any of that. I was too wrapped up in my feelings for Pierre and thinking that alone held the key to news that would change his life forever."

"I understand everything you're saying, Roz, but I'm not going to help you fall on the sword. I still maintain that had Andy more respect for your talent, perspective and overall working relationship, he would have never released that story. Had he a conscience or thread of moral decency, he would not have allowed it to run without giving Pierre a heads-up, at the very least. Sure, if given a second chance there are things you would have done differently. But you did not write nor publish that article. That part of the equation, the most important and damaging, is not on you. It's on Andy, Paige and *NO Beat*."

"Thanks, Stef. It doesn't necessarily help me feel better, but in time I'll probably come around to that point of view. Tonight I'm full into pity partying, mud wallowing and telling myself I'm the worst kind of friend."

"Just as you feel your actions make you disloyal, his actions toward you make him an A-hole."

"Stef—"

"My opinion's not up for discussion."

"Like I said, I'll probably come back to pissed off later. But not tonight."

"Continue dancing with the doldrums if you must, but I'm going to let that be at a party of one. We have a photo shoot tomorrow with the model from hell. It'll probably last all day. I'll need a good night's sleep, an hour of yoga and placement on Mom's prayer list just to get through it."

Roz laughed in spite of having labeled herself a disloyal girlfriend, and her goal to feel appropriately miserable. "You'll be amazing, as always. And, hey. Tell your mom to put me and my situation on that prayer list, too."

Chapter 26

For the second time in three days, Pierre pulled his car up to Roz's house. The first time was Monday night after talking with Ma. Even though it was late, he'd left her humble abode determined to apologize for his actions and share with Roz what else was on his mind. But he'd arrived at a house that was dark save for a dim light coming from her bedroom. He'd lost the nerve to disturb her and had gone home instead. Yesterday, Lisette had called with news that further upset him. It had easily been the most contentious conversation the close siblings had ever had. That experience, and his continued unsettled feelings for Roz, made for little sleep.

Pierre was used to a hectic lifestyle, but he knew this kind of stress could not be maintained. Which was why Wednesday night found him once again looking for a place to park his SUV near Roz's vintage bungalow. He pulled in on a side street, just around the corner from her front door. Once on the sidewalk he was relieved to see a light on in her living room. She was home and still awake. He stood there a moment, trying to think of a way to apologize and stay strong. She'd be angry. A deserved reaction, given the way he'd acted. After that night in the courtyard she'd sent a text saying she understood his outrage and still wanted to talk. He hadn't responded. She hadn't tried again. The next time they'd seen each other was the other night at Ma's. Remembering how he'd acted there gave him even less confidence to knock on her door.

"Nothing's going to happen with me dawdling here," he mumbled, finally stepping forward. He rang the doorbell. Waited. Rang it again. Waited longer this time.

A thought occurred to him. *What if she's with some-one?* It was a possibility he'd not considered. One that made him want to race to his car on one hand and break down the door on the other. He tried the screen door. It was unlocked. He opened it and knocked—actually banged, pounded—on the wooden front door. He heard Banner's ferocious barking, imagined him jumping toward the door, ready to charge the assailant. Just as Pierre raised his fist to knock again, the door was jerked open.

"I tried the doorbell," he said, as if to explain the incessant pounding. "Sorry to come by unannounced."

"Then why did you?" Roz demanded, as she wrestled to control a barking Yorkie squirming to get out of her arms.

"Didn't think I'd get an invitation had I called." He looked at Banner and tried to lighten the situation. "Doesn't look like I'm too welcomed now."

Roz's expression made it clear that the attempt didn't work.

"May I come in?"

"It's late."

"What I have to say won't take long."

"You don't think you've said enough already?"

Obviously, or I wouldn't be here. A thought not verbalized as he met Roz's steely mahogany eyes with his own turbulent stare. He braced himself for having the door slammed in his face and breathed a sigh of relief when she turned, released Banner and walked into the living room. Pierre followed her. When she reached the middle of the room, she turned around, crossed arms serving as armor. Expecting a fight.

"Okay. You're in. What is it?"

"I see you're not going to make this easy." He shoved clammy hands into his jeans pockets. Forced his breathing to remain slow and easy. "I'm sorry."

He watched those two words wash over her, ease a bit of the stiffness in her back. Just a little.

"I am sorry for not hearing you out, for all of the accusations and quick judgment. Knowing you the way I do, it should have been obvious that there was more to the story than what I assumed. I'm sorry for the other day. Said a lot of stuff that I can't take back. That in hindsight I didn't mean. I had over a decade of anger and hurt inside of me and it exploded on you."

"You had every right to be angry. What happened was my fault."

"But you didn't write the article."

"No, but I inspired the curiosity that led to my sources being deceived and the story breaking. Which is why I'm no longer there."

"You quit your job?"

"I couldn't work for someone who'd do that to me, to anybody."

"Who'd deceive you, right?"

Roz nodded.

"Then I still don't understand how what happened is your fault."

"I should have taken time off and flown to LA on my own dime. But I didn't." Roz broke eye contact and sat on a nearby chair.

Pierre walked to the couch, asking a question with his eyes. Roz nodded. He sat down.

"*NO Beat* flew me out with the purpose of getting a story, which I fully intended to do. My plan, however, was to verify what I'd heard, share that information with you and then write a piece that incorporated both your and Alana's perspectives. Kind of a follow-up to your earlier story in the 'Where Are They Now?' series. One that I hoped would point to a happy ending. Your reaction changed all of that. I returned to work and flat-out refused to write the article or even share what I'd learned. My boss wasn't happy. I knew that, but underestimated his determination to uncover what I'd worked so hard to hide."

"How'd he find out?"

"By using the only information I was willing to share before going to LA—that someone thought to have died in Hurricane Katrina was actually very much alive and living there."

"Definitely sounds like a juicy story."

"The potential of what could be and ultimately was uncovered are what award-winning stories are made of— mystery, intrigue, drama, possible scandal. All of the questions. Who is this person? How'd they survive? Why did they leave and, as important or perhaps more so, why did they not come back?"

"All the questions they're asking now, or so I've heard."

"You talked to her?" Roz asked, shock evident in her voice.

Pierre shook his head. "Lizzy. She went to meet her. She's there now."

"I can't imagine you'd be happy about that."

"Not at all. We had a pretty big fight about it. Then I remembered the words of a very wise woman and called her back. Apologized. Told her that Alana was her mother and this was her life, and she had to handle what happened in the way that worked best for her."

"Wow, that's a one-eighty turnaround. Who was this woman?"

Pierre looked over and offered a tentative smile. "Ma."

Roz nodded. She totally understood. "Thank you for the

apology. I own my part in all of this, but your harshness the other night was incredibly hurtful, and unexpected."

"I know. In that moment, I transferred the hurt I'd felt on to you." He stood and walked over to the window. "After Mom died…left… I never trusted women. Not after she promised to meet us in Houston and didn't. For a kid who'd never really known his father, and who'd dealt with other lies, half-truths and disappointments, it was especially damaging. Definitely a last straw for my fifteen-year-old self when it came to women and credibility."

Pierre turned around. "Then I met you."

"Pierre…"

He held up a hand to silence her. "It's okay. Let me finish." He returned to the couch. "I didn't want to trust you. When I found you so easy to talk to I became even more wary, telling myself that it was journalistic skill, not concern that made you sound genuine. In a very short time that feeling changed. The more I opened up the more appreciative I was of having someone like you to talk to, to share my feelings with instead of keeping them bottled up inside. I've always had Lizzy, but there are some things you can't share with your baby sis. So when I felt that trust had been broken, it almost broke me."

"I'm so sorry,"

"My pain isn't your fault. Not the deep ache that finding out Alana was alive has evoked. I had a scab over that wound. What happened between us snatched it off. That's what happened."

"I get that." They became silent, both aware of the atmosphere shifting. Of the emotional wall between them dissipating. Of their being able to really see the other again.

"You gave Lisette the number?" he finally asked.

"To her mom?" There was a pause as Pierre imagined Roz weighing the repercussion of her answer. "Yes, I did."

He nodded. "Good."

Her eyebrows rose at the same time that her mouth dropped open. "Really?"

"Yes, as hard as it is for me to say it, Lizzy reconnecting with her mother has been good for her. Challenging, yes. Painful, too. But she's glad to have found her. Glad she's alive."

"That has to be hard for you, given you've been all Lisette has had for all these years. A huge responsibility."

"A part of me felt that I was all she needed. That it was me and baby girl against the world. But a daughter needs her mother."

"And you?" Roz softly asked.

"Ma knew Alana."

"No way."

"I was shocked, too. Actually, she knew Grand-Mère, and…my mom…by extension. Knew her way better than I ever did. Some of what she shared filled in blanks, gave me a more complete perspective."

"What did she say?"

"I'll tell you later. Right now, I want to tell you how much I've missed you. How my world has seemed a bit dimmer, and colder, without you in it."

"I've missed you, too."

"I'm happy to hear that. I want to thank you, too."

"For?"

"Finding my grandmother's remains. Lisette told me that when I arrived back in the States, but with everything going on, the news was barely heard and quickly forgotten."

"It's okay. Took a phone call and two minutes."

"Whatever it took, you did it. Thank you. Now we can at least get closure for her."

"You're welcome. I was happy to help."

"Baby, I can't believe you quit your job over what they did to me."

"Well, I did."

"That leaves me speechless. I don't think anyone has ever stood up for me like that. What are you going to do?"

"I don't know." She raised a brow. "You hiring?"

"Maybe. Can you wash dishes?"

Roz and Pierre shared a laugh as the discomfort between them lessened and camaraderie began to flow. Soon, conversation led to caresses, then kisses, then new positions in places they'd never tried. Pierre knew all she'd done for his family deserved a special kind of thank-you. Until that could happen, for a good part of the night, he used his body to demonstrate how he felt, and how much Roz was appreciated.

Chapter 27

The distinct smell of bacon tickled his nose. Pierre frowned, turned over, confused that he could dream so realistically he smelled odors, while feeling half-awake. A few seconds—or was it minutes or hours—later, his senses were assaulted again. This time it was the delicious combination of cinnamon and nutmeg that caused him to inhale, reach out for Roz and feel the cold side of her bed. Lifting his still weary head from the pillow, he slowly opened his eyes to the vision of Roz in a sheer purple nightie that reached her thighs, and nothing else, carrying a tray as she entered the room.

"What's this?" He seated himself against the headboard and pulled the sheet around him.

"Breakfast." She positioned the tray over his legs, and added a quick peck before stepping back and away from him.

"You cook?"

"That description would be generous. Mom doesn't cook, but felt it necessary to master one dish of each meal, in case of an emergency, like the cook getting sick or another Katrina. This is my go-to breakfast."

Pierre picked up a slice of the thick slab bacon and examined it. "Perfectly crisp," he noted, "while leaving a bit of the fat moist and tender." He bit off almost half the slice, cut a piece of French toast and added that to his mouth. He closed his eyes, nodding as he chewed. "This is delicious, Roz."

"You really think so?" Excitement from his compliment shone in her eyes.

"I've eaten my share of French toast and this is a worthy representation of the dish. I taste the cinnamon and just a tad of nutmeg and cloves, present but not overpowering. Is there caramel in the syrup?"

Roz nodded. "It's made by slowly melting caramel chunks into pure maple syrup. I'd like to say I grew the fruit in your bowl and picked it myself, but that came from a grocery store container."

She left to make a second helping of toast for Pierre and a plate for herself. She poured two large glasses of orange juice and then rejoined him in bed.

"Thanks, babe." Pierre dug into his second helping of toast with gusto, bringing another wide smile to Roz's face. "You know, I just realized something."

"Hmm?" Roz murmured, still chewing.

"In all the time we've known each other you've learned quite a bit about my family, but I don't know much about yours."

"My history is not nearly as exciting."

"Perhaps, but it is definitely above average."

"How do you know?"

"Average homes do not employ cooks."

"I'd label my family as…interesting."

"How so?"

Roz took a few more bites, then reached for her drink. "From the outside looking in, the Arnauds are an upstanding, successful, close-knit, beautiful family. That's mostly true. My dad's a judge. His brother an attorney who worked in the president's administration during his second term. My mother is one of the most illustrious socialites in the city, who made sure we wore the right labels, drove the right cars and lived in the proper zip code. What was and still is lacking are those intangibles that make a house feel homey."

"Such as?"

"Warmth, open displays of affection. The easy cama- raderie and relaxed comfort I experienced in other homes I visited while growing up. That I enjoyed at Stefanie's house when helping her mom clip coupons or watching her dad and brother yelling at the television during football games. The lived-in atmosphere of messy rooms, dusty shelves, worn carpets and red Kool-Aid stains on lami- nate countertops.

"My mom is a perfectionist and all about appearances. She is also a proud Southern Creole belle who was crowned queen at her debutante ball. She loves and lives for teas and charities, spa sessions and international shopping dates with friends. I didn't embrace that world at all, and for her that was a huge disappointment. I didn't want to live in a society that chose my friends and set my standards. She wanted me to attend Tulane, but Daddy, who I'm closer to and more like, saw past my fake smile to the misery that lay beneath, and rescued me with the notion of expanding my cultural experiences with a Midwestern education."

"And look at what happened. You turned out beautifully."

"Thank you."

"The same can't be said for my mom."

Roz placed her plate on the tray and moved it to the nightstand. "Was hers a similar childhood?"

Pierre made a sound. "Hardly, but there is a similarity. Mom wasn't close to Grand-Mère either. Wasn't until re- cently that I found out why."

"Is this what Ma shared the other night?"

He nodded. "According to her, Mom was the product of an affair my grandmother had with a married man, one she believed was the love of her life. It's crazy because Grand-

Mère was strict, a staunch Catholic who like your mother felt appearance was everything. I guess she justified her actions by the fact that they planned to be married, and once that happened, any sin could be absolved. He led her on for years, saying he'd leave his wife. Whether she got pregnant by accident or as a way to hasten his divorce, Ma didn't know. But shortly after her birth, he broke it off for good. Ma said Grand-Mère blamed Alana for losing him. She was a baby. How was it her fault?"

Roz shook her head.

"Ma said Grand-Mère was very hard on Mom. That instead of being loved, Mom was tolerated. When she was twelve or thirteen, Grand-Mère married a man who was even stricter than she was, who would beat Alana for the slightest perceived wrong. My mom couldn't understand how Grand-Mère could allow that from someone who wasn't even her father. But she did. It caused a rift that never healed.

"When the incidents continued, Mom ran away. That's when she met my father, a man ten years older with a handsome face, a convincing line and an apartment."

"How old was your mom?"

"The same age I was when she left me," Pierre said, turning to look at her. "Fifteen."

"Is that when she got pregnant?"

"No. That happened a year or so later, a few months shy of her seventeenth birthday."

"Wow. It doesn't absolve your mother for abandoning you but…"

"It makes me a little more understanding of how she could do it. Gave me the ability to stop hating her, to forgive her as Lisette has done. Especially after hearing the rest of the story."

Roz said nothing, just scooted over and placed her head on his shoulder. He hugged her closer to his side.

"Mom stayed with my dad for several years, only leaving when she met Lizzy's father, who promised her the moon on a platter and the stars in a stemmed glass. Like the one she'd just gotten out of, this was another controlling, abusive relationship. Ma wasn't sure how it ended, but could only imagine Alana's lack of self-esteem after years of mental, emotional and physical abuse."

"Do you remember any of that?"

"The arguments for sure, and how her personality changed when Glen was around."

"Lizzy's father?"

Pierre nodded. "Mom was outgoing, but when he came home she'd get quiet, mousy, rushing here and there to do his bidding. Thinking back, I remember the times when they'd be in their bedroom and I heard things. Noises that in retrospect could have been caused by physical violence. I guess it was her attempt to shield us from what was happening. Which was probably best. Several of my friends owned guns and I know how to use them. I would never have let anyone continue hurting my mom."

"I take it you didn't get along with your stepfather."

"History repeated itself. Both Lizzy and I were barely tolerated. It was clear that he didn't like kids, and definitely didn't like any attention Mom gave us when he was around. Mom moved out when I was seven and Lizzy was three, but they were together off and on for the next four, five years. Things got worse, especially the physical violence, which always happened when I wasn't around. Mom tried to hide it but I knew, and I told her what I planned to do about it. She broke up with him for good a couple years before Katrina, but he continued to stalk, threaten and harass her up until the levees broke.

"In meeting that doctor she may have felt like those Katrina flood victims pulled into life rafts from rooftops. That she was being pulled from a hurricane of heartache on what might be the only boat to come her way."

Later that day, as Pierre headed to work, his phone rang.

"Hey, sis. Are you still in LA.?"

"Yes."

"Did you move there?"

Lizzy laughed. "I want to! Flying home on Friday. Did you get the pictures?"

"What pictures?"

"The ones I sent just now of me, Mom, her husband, Bernard, and our sister, Chloe."

That he didn't stiffen at the mention of his half sister was proof of how fast love and forgiveness could heal the soul.

"No, I'm driving."

"Call me back when you see them. Chloe looks more like your sister than I do!" Lizzy paused, then added, "Mom really wants to see you, Pierre. She understands why you're mad and hates what she did, but if you would at least talk to her—"

"Okay."

"And give her a chance to explain why she did what she did and how she always planned to come back for us, but then she got pregnant and...wait. Did you say okay?"

"With your nonstop rambling, I'm surprised you heard it," Pierre said, with a smile in his voice.

"You mean it? I can give her your number and if she calls you'll pick up?"

"If I have time to talk I will, and if not, I'll call her back."

"Pear, you sound totally different. What happened to change your mind?"

"A woman named Ma. And another one named Rosalyn."

They talked a little longer before he ended the call. Not five minutes later another one came in, with an area code he didn't recognize.

"LeBlanc."

"Pierre."

His heart leaped and caught in his throat as a flurry of feelings assailed him. Tears, unexpected and unbidden, misted his eyes.

"It's your mom."

"I recognized the voice," he said, clearing a throat suddenly raspy with emotion.

"I love you, Pierre."

"I know."

"I'm so happy to talk to you. Over the years I've had a thousand conversations—so much to share, so much I wanted to know. And now, hearing your voice, I'm speechless. Thank you so much for taking my call. To say that I'm sorry is a gross understatement. We can't turn back time, but if you'll let me, I'll spend the rest of my life trying to make up for all the years you spent without me, and all the hurt and pain I caused by leaving your life.

"I'm so sorry, Pierre. Can you ever forgive me?"

"I forgive you, Mom, especially because Lizzy sounds so happy. But I can't completely forget what you did, even as I now can better understand why. I can't act like those years didn't happen. But I will try and get past what they did to my psyche, and to my soul."

"Son, I would love to see you and will do anything to regain your love and your trust. Anything you ask."

"Then I ask for time. I know everyone wants this instant, Hallmark moment, and one of these days I'll probably be ready to see you again. But I'm not there yet."

Chapter 28

Roz was cautiously optimistic. For the past week, since making up with Pierre, they'd experienced a closer connection than she'd ever imagined. Spending every available moment together. Finishing each other's sentences. Anticipating the other's physical need before it was verbalized. Pierre made love to her like none other. Was this what soul mates felt like?

The only thing missing from her picture-perfect world was a J-O-B. She'd sent résumés to every media outlet in the state, and while getting a few nibbles, not one in-person interview had been scheduled. Stefanie had suggested she cast a wider net. Look into larger nearby markets such as Dallas, Houston, Atlanta or Miami. Roz had thought about Midwestern markets such as Kansas City or Saint Louis, where she still kept in touch with ex-classmates and teachers. Not long ago she would have jumped at the chance to broaden her experience and increase her earning potential through diverse employment. Now all she could think of was what a relocation would mean…being away from Pierre.

This was on her mind as the cell phone rang with what she hoped was a bona fide request for a job interview. She looked at the zip code. Houston, she thought. Great! Within driving distance, close to Lisette and where Pierre used to live.

"Good afternoon!"

"Yes, hello. I'm looking to speak with Roz Arnaud, please."

"Speaking."

"Roz, hi. It's Lana Stern."

The unexpected announcement caught her totally off guard.

"Alana?"

"If you insist. However, my name has been legally changed to Lana Juliette Stern. I'd prefer to be called by the name I use now."

"Of course, Alana. I mean Lana. Sorry for sounding flustered. This call is a surprise and the absolute last one I expected to receive, especially with a Houston area code."

"That's 7-1-3. My prefix, 7-1-4, is a code for Orange County."

"Oh."

"I'm glad to know that you aren't the only one with surprises or a trick or two up your sleeve."

"I'm not sure what you mean."

"Never mind. Any ill intentions you may have had in seeking me out have been circumvented by my daughter's reaction and desire to see me. You probably know that she recently came here and enjoyed a wonderful visit. One of the reasons I'm calling is to thank you for that."

"You're quite welcome, and for the record, the only intention I had initially was finding your remains to give Pierre and Lisette some type of clarifying closure. When I was told you were alive my second intention was to confirm that. Once that had been done, I only wanted to tell Pierre and let him dictate what happened from there."

"Is that why they pulled the story from you and gave it to the other girl?"

"The story wasn't pulled, it was stolen. I refused to run it or give them Pierre's name. The paper went behind my back, mined my sources and ran the story over my strong objection."

"They told me you were fired for sleeping with Pierre."

"I wasn't fired at all. I quit."

"Because they ran the story?"

"Yes, and because of the methods they used to obtain the information. There were integrity and character issues that came into question, which left me unable to continue employment there."

"Are you and my son dating?"

"Yes."

"Do you love him?"

"Alana, excuse my bluntness, but what is this call about?"

"I'm sorry. It's just that I know so little about him, really, only what I've read in magazines and online. That is another reason for my call, to apologize."

"For what?"

"For my behavior when you found me. I was shocked and scared and hid all of that behind a mask of confidence and sophistication that in the circles I now travel I've learned to wear well. Inside I was praying that your visit would somehow lead to a reunion with my kids, and it did. Lisette is everything and much more than I ever imagined. Having her here brought back parts of me that I didn't know were gone. It's a reconciliation that is long overdue."

"You followed them online for years. There were any number of chances to fly to where they lived and end their pain years ago."

"I know, and I will never forgive myself for being such a coward. Instead of me taking the lead as a mother should, I waited for one of my children to call me. That happened because of you. That's why I'm thanking you, and is the final reason for my call. Lisette says that you and Pierre really love each other. And while my actions suggest otherwise, I love them both with all my heart.

"Here's what's really at the crux of this request. Lisette is a Christmas baby. Her birthday is on December 23. When she was in LA she mentioned more than once that her dream was for all of us to sit down to dinner—my husband and daughter, her and Pierre—all together, like a real family. I would love to make that dream coming true her surprise birthday gift, and I can't think of a better place for it to happen than my son's restaurant. I've asked to see him and so has Lisette. So far he's refused. But I know how it is when a woman has a man's heart. She can get him to do things that others can't."

"Don't you think being ready to see you is a decision for Pierre to make, not something to be forced on him through a birthday request?"

"Probably. But it would make my daughter so happy, and yes, I'd love it, too."

"There will be other years and more birthdays."

"I know." There was a pause, during which Roz detected...a sniffle? Was Alana crying? "For all these years I've kept my feelings for my children under lock and key. It was the only way I could stay sane. But seeing Lisette and talking to Pierre has broken my heart open. Seeing my daughter gave me back part of myself, and restored parts of her. I believe that would happen with Pierre, too. I don't deserve it, but I want the chance to begin again. Starting with seeing him in person, and asking, begging forgiveness from the boy who I forced to become a man."

There was no doubt that Alana was crying now. Roz heard the tears in her voice.

"Roz, do you have children?"

"No, I don't."

"If you ever do, then you'll have some idea of how a mother loves her child, how deeply and completely, unconditionally and forever. I left them, but I never stopped loving them. A mother doesn't stop loving, no matter what. The designer clothes and expensive jewels cover a heart that has been broken since the day I put those kids on the bus. I know it's hard to believe that, but it's true. Pierre is very angry with me. He probably hates me. I deserve to be hated. I don't blame him at all. Nevertheless I want the chance to see him, to hug him. I want the chance to make my daughter's dream come true. I want the chance to begin making up what can never be made up. To repay what can never be given back. But I want to try. Roz, I have absolutely no right to ask…"

"I'll talk to him," she said softly. Not because of what Alana said, but because of what Roz felt for the very first time—what was totally hidden when they'd met in person—Alana's heart.

Hours into nonstop work, with diners occupying every available table, Pierre still grappled with the conversation he'd had with his mother, and the opposing emotions the conversation had created. He envied Lisette's singular, unabashed joy, how she could reach out and accept their mother's love as though nothing had happened. Could fly out to visit, embrace their half sister with no hesitation and take family pictures with all of them as though it wasn't her first time.

Before leaving his car he'd called and told her that he and Alana had talked. Lizzy had broken down, crying. Happy tears, she confirmed. She wanted to know everything—what they'd talked about, how soon he would meet her. So convinced that he'd fall back in love with their mom, when he'd spoken of his hesitancy to meet her, Lisette wasn't disappointed. She was happy to know they had talked at all.

Pierre could understand her elation. Having anything to do with his mother hadn't been an option as recently as just three days ago. Talking on the phone had been emotionally grueling. What would happen if he saw her in person? In his mind he'd forgiven her, but would the angry beast reemerge with them in the same room? That was the question being pondered as he entered the kitchen.

Once there, though, his focus shifted to his baby, Easy Creole Cuisine, and the life he'd built without having a mom around to guide, encourage and motivate him. What did she think of everything he'd accomplished? Would she have been as eager to meet them were he and his sister not successful? If Lisette wasn't smart and beautiful and he wasn't famous and rich? A part of him wanted to believe those were ludicrous questions. They came nonetheless, wanting to be answered. And there were more. About his father, and Lisette's. Her childhood and the scars it left. And in having been at least emotionally abandoned herself, how had it been possible for Alana to turn around and abandon her children?

After taking an hour to handle business with his agent, Pierre reentered the restaurant sanctuary otherwise known as the kitchen, relieved to shift his focus back to work. Four months in and the Easy kitchen was running better than expected. Pierre wasn't surprised. He'd consulted Marc often, had organized his kitchen exactly how he'd been taught at New Orleans. Hiring employees for the front of the house had been fairly easy, but knowing how much turnover took place in kitchens, he'd offered competitive salaries and been meticulous in selecting a back-of-the-house staff that he could train to his standards and keep for the long-term. No one could know how long it would last, but as Pierre inspected the work of each cook and station, he liked what he saw. He loved the teamwork vibe. In time, he'd have to reconcile his feelings regarding his mother. It was neither healthy nor productive to forgive, then still harbor feelings that made true healing incomplete.

Every chair in the main dining room was reserved, with special guests for the private rooms, too. Riviera, the exceptional sous chef, was running the orders for the early dinner service. The appropriate cook would echo back the order, insuring everyone working was on the same page and no item was missed.

"Alright, family, listen up. We've got two Cajun steaks—one medium, one rare."

"Two steaks. Mid. Light."

"Three blackened catfish, two smothered pork chops."

"Three black cats, three wet pigs all day!"

Pierre joined several others who laughed at the station cook's unique interpretations.

"Two jambalaya, two shrimp étouffées."

"Two jams, two shrimp eats!"

"Heard, Chef!"

"Everyone got that?" Pierre asked.

"Yes, Chef!"

About halfway through the early dinner service, one of the servers entered the kitchen. Unusual in that they normally stood at the pass.

It was Lisa, a quiet, highly efficient young mother of two. "Excuse me, Chef. There's someone outside wanting to speak with you, Roz Arnaud. She said it's important."

Roz?

"Lisa, direct her to the side door."

"Yes, Chef."

"Riviera, can you handle the stove?"

"Got it, Chef."

"Be right back."

Pierre peeled off his apron and tossed it aside. His heart raced even though he told himself to stay calm. Hard to do. They'd kissed each other goodbye mere hours ago. What was so important that couldn't be texted, so time-sensitive that she'd come by work?

He opened the door and quickly pulled Roz inside. "What's wrong?" He continued down the hall to his office at the end. Closing the door, he asked again, more urgently, "Tell me, Roz. What's wrong?"

"Pierre, I'm sorry. Nothing's wrong."

"But you told Lisa it was important. What couldn't wait until I got off work?"

"It's about your mom. And Lisette."

Pierre crossed his arms and waited. With his wide-legged stance and fierce arched-brow glower, he felt like a commanding gladiator daring any foe to enter the ring.

Brave Roz took a step forward. "This won't take long, but please hear me all the way out before saying anything or making a decision. When Lisette was in LA, she shared a dream with your mom. It was for all of you to be together, at one time, in one place. Lana wants to make that happen as a surprise for Lisette's birthday. She called and shared the idea with me in hopes that I could help bring it about. The only reason I came right away is because your restaurant's always booked and Lisette's birthday is next week."

A couple seconds went by. "Are you finished?"

Roz nodded. "I'm sorry for coming to your workplace. She called about an hour ago and the more I thought about it, the more I felt you needed to know right away. I know how much you love Lisette and if anything would make you see Lana, fulfilling a dream for Lisette would probably be it."

"Lizzy's dream, or Alana's?"

"Your mom said it was Lisette's dream and I believe her."

Pierre scowled, unconvinced. "Feels like manipulation and that's not in my sister's toolbox."

"Would you like me to try and find out from Lisette myself?"

Pierre remained silent.

"It sounded to me like a comment made during a general conversation. Lisette didn't suggest that it happen on her birthday. That much was Lana's idea. Because of how much it seemed to mean to Lisette, she thought it would be a great birthday gift. So just to be clear, the desire to see you all together is your sister's. For it to happen next week is your mom's. That's it. I've delivered the message so my conscience is now clear."

She rose up and kissed Pierre's jaw, then whispered in his ear, "Follow your heart, babe. Don't let anyone pressure you. And don't pressure yourself. I'll let myself back out the side door."

Pierre watched Roz leave and after more than five minutes of hard thinking reached for his phone and sent Lisette a text.

Hey Lizzy, just thought about your birthday coming up. What do you want?

She responded within seconds.

My whole family together.

Pierre's response was equally fast.

What's your second choice?

Chapter 29

December 23 fell on a Monday, making Roz's part in planning Lisette's twenty-fifth birthday party easy to execute. She'd asked Lisette's favorite color, red, then convinced the recent graduate student to leave the rest of the night's festivities up to her. Roz promised not to disappoint. The week that followed was the only time she was grateful for still being unemployed. It took working every day, for upward of ten to twelve hours at a time to pull off an evening that Lisette wouldn't forget. Roz couldn't guarantee Liz's birthday dream, but between her and Pierre's connections, Lisette would have an incredibly enjoyable night.

Roz pulled into the parking lot across from Easy Creole Cuisine and was relieved to see Stefanie's pearl-white Hyundai Sonata. She exited her car with phone in hand, sending last-minute instructions to the baker finishing Lisette's birthday cake. Stefanie was on the phone, too, but finished the call as she reached her.

"Hey, Biff."

They shared a brief hug. "Hey, Biff, I'm glad you're here."

Roz hurried across the street. Stefanie worked to keep up.

"What are we doing?"

"Meeting with the company lighting the room, the Christmas tree decorator, the DJ and—" Roz scrolled down a list on her smartphone "—confirming that King Sir is still going to come through and sing 'Happy Birthday.'"

Stefanie had stopped in the middle of the street. Roz turned around. "What are you doing? Come on!"

"Are you kidding? King Sir is going to be there tonight?"

"Yes, come on!"

"You cannot tell me that someone as big as the King is coming somewhere that I'm not invited, and expect me to act normal. *King Sir?*"

"Come on, girl. You're not invited directly but you know I'll get you in, tell Pierre you're the cake cutter or something."

They went inside. An hour later, Roz felt like an honorary fireman putting out one blaze after another. Wrong cake flavor. Decorations incomplete. And she'd just finished arguing with the popular radio station DJ booked to play Lisette's party, who wanted to cut his time in half and play only one hour. As she sent Stefanie over to handle the botched cake order while she secured another decorator, Roz could only hope and pray that the meeting Pierre had scheduled went better than her day.

Almost an hour late to a meeting set up less than eight hours ago, Pierre's leather-gloved hands deftly navigated almost thirty-five hundred pounds of biturbo horsepower through relatively light midday traffic on Interstate 10. Partly cloudy skies made the day feel colder than the sixty-one degrees registered on the car's dash. Still, he drove with the top down, the heater up and the stereo blasting "Birdland" by Weather Report. Black buffalo-horn Cartier shades hid an uncertain gaze from eyes red-tinged by lack of sleep. A black wool turtleneck, black jeans and black-and-tan Fendi goat leather slip-ons matched his Ferrari's smooth black exterior, while soft tan leather caressed his equally tanned skin. Eyes followed the handsome man in the shiny car from the highway to the exit and now Canal Street, but Pierre didn't notice. His mind was filled with other things, making Lizzy's party perfect among them.

Pulling up to the valet sign, Pierre raised the top, spoke

to the uniformed attendant and walked inside the Ritz-Carlton. He cut a fine figure as he crossed the expansive lobby with its creamy marble floors and ornate chandeliers, and reached a bank of elevators. He stepped inside one and pushed the button for the fourteenth floor, resting his head against the cool wall as memories assailed him. Too soon the ride ended, but Pierre's steps were sure as he searched the walls for the suite number he'd been given. Seconds later, with a light tap and an opened door, the whole earth shifted.

"Pierre." The word came out on an anguished breath, through trembling lips in a face strained with uncertainty.

"Mom." He stood there, planted to the floor as a tsunami of emotions swept through him. At once he was the toddler who clung endlessly to a mother's bare leg. The kid who stole lavender irises from a neighbor's yard for her birthday. The teen who'd refused to look back on a bus bound for Houston. The man who stared into eyes so like his own. The son who still loved his mother.

His eyes skittered from the pain of hers to hands clenched tightly together. Hands that slowly opened, shaky arms that raised and stretched, offering a hug. Pierre stepped stiffly into her embrace. The one arm he wrapped around her waist was less for affection and more to keep him standing upright.

"Oh, son!" His mother's breath warmed his ear as she crushed herself against him. "Pierre, baby, I'm so sorry. I'm so sorry I left you. I'm sorry for everything."

She continued to cry and mumble. Tears streamed down her face as she placed a hand on each side of his and stared into his eyes. Pierre stood still, his own eyes shimmering with unshed tears. Inside, he screamed with relief at seeing his mother's pretty face. A bit older, her hair shorter and lighter, but otherwise basically the same as he remembered. His heart nearly burst with the emotion of the moment. But he held these feelings in a masculine grip of fear and pride. He'd loved this woman with his whole heart once, and it had been broken.

"It's hard to let go of you for even a moment." With a final squeeze, Lana stepped back. "Please, come in."

Pierre entered the lavishly appointed room with wrap-around windows that took in the French Quarter. Ironically, his restaurant was just beyond its view, rather like his mother had been from his for the past fourteen, almost fifteen years. He crossed the sitting room and looked curiously into the bedroom on his way to the windows.

"They're out, Bernie and Chloe, taking in the sights. It's her first time here and I wanted this moment to be just between us." Pierre continued to stare out the window. He wanted to stare at her, but to do so might break him. "Would you like to sit down?"

"I don't have much time. I'm on my way to the restaurant to prepare for the party."

"You can't begin to know how proud I am of you."

He gave a sarcastic chuckle. "No, I can't."

"I've followed everything you've done since you went on TV. Once I found Lisette online, I followed her, too. Like a voyeur, scavenging the internet for every scrap of news I could find on the two of you. You raised yourself and your sister better than I ever could, had I stayed here. What you've done on your own is beyond anything I could have—"

"Why didn't you come back?" Pierre spun around, his eyes boring into her with unflinching ire. "You found Grand-Mère dead. It shook you up. I get that. Life was hard for you here and when you had the chance to escape, you took it. I get that, too. But why didn't you come back?"

Pierre's voice became firmer, louder, as he crossed to where Lana sat. "After arriving in the city of champagne wishes and caviar dreams, after getting a home and a husband and having a child and making a life…"

His eyes glistened, but he dared tears to fall. The weight of the moment was so heavy Pierre's legs could not hold him. He sat in the chair facing her, his voice now raw, low. "Why didn't you come find us? Or even call? All those years that you saw us online. It never occurred to you to send a letter, an email, a tweet? To reach out to your children, the ones you abandoned? Why did you let us believe you were dead for all these years? Throw us to the wolves and leave us to fend for ourselves or get eaten alive?"

Lana reached for a tissue and dabbed at tears that refused to stop flowing. "I understand your questions, Pierre, and I wish I could answer them. But, baby, there is no answer, no reason that would justify what I did to you and Liz. The woman who left New Orleans was frightened, weak, broken. Bernie's offer to take me with him felt like a lifeline, not only from Katrina, but from the flood of failures that was my life. I didn't tell him I had children. Given what had been happening with me and Liz's dad, I was afraid to tell him, afraid that he'd leave me there in that mental ward. And I felt that if he left me there, I'd never walk out on my own. I convinced myself that it was okay to leave you with relatives. Told myself it was just until I got settled and found the right time to tell Bernie about you."

"But the right time never came."

Lana shook her head. "Life moved so fast. Everything happened so quickly. My mind spinning with new places and people and a completely new, totally foreign way of life. I was terrified of failing again. Determined to erase the struggling, abused teenaged mom and become the sophisticated doctor's wife that Bernie deserved. In the middle of that chaotic, terrifying first year, I learned I was pregnant. I came the closest to telling him then. One night as we lay in bed and he shared his happiness at becoming a dad. He was already forty-nine by then and resigned to never having children."

"Why didn't you?"

"I couldn't. Too risky, I thought. Too much to lose. I'd tell him after the baby… There was always a reason and at the same time there was no reason ever good enough. The more time passed, the bigger the lie became in my mind. Then when I found you two online and saw how well you were doing, amazingly really, I thought it better that you didn't know. Again, I don't know why I felt that way, Pierre, but I did. I didn't feel worthy of being in the life of someone so amazing as you. So handsome and talented, with such a big heart. One that helped his sister be successful, too.

"I don't know what will happen after tonight. More than a decade of pain and neglect can't be wiped out in a moment. But I want to thank you for coming here, letting me see you and hold you and smell you like I did when you were a baby. And for going out of your way to make Lisette happy. She's going to be over the moon."

The door opened. A kindly looking older man with salt-and-pepper curls and an authoritative demeanor stood there, clearly surprised to see Pierre was still present.

"I'm sorry, hon," he said to Lana, his warm brown eyes sending love that could be felt across the room.

Behind him the lively chatter of two teens faded as they entered, saw Pierre and Lana, and stopped behind Bernard.

Lana looked at Pierre.

"It's okay," he told her, as he took in a tall, lanky beauty who looked more like him than Lisette did, just as she'd told him.

Introductions were made, a bit awkward but not hostile. When Pierre left moments later, Lana asked to hug him again. He gave her permission, and this time, he hugged her back.

Chapter 30

Roz pulled in front of the valet stand at Pierre's restaurant. The wheels had barely stopped rolling before a handsome young man with bright eyes and a sincere smile stepped up and opened her door.

"Good evening, ma'am. Welcome to Easy Creole Cuisine."

"Thank you."

"You look beautiful tonight."

Roz opened her mouth to protest, swallowed the objection and matched his smile. "Thanks."

She smoothed her dress's velvety fabric over her stomach more to quell a sudden case of nerves than anything else. It was crazy to be anxious. In a twist of fate, she'd been not only the catalyst for this dinner happening tonight, but the grand event's premiere planner. She knew that everything inside the small private room was now perfect. That the floor had been covered with furry white carpeting. Deep red covers transformed the chairs and were secured with wide iridescent, beaded bows. The twelve-foot tree that anchored the corner opposite the room's entrance was also decorated with Lisette's favorite color—in bling. The boxes beneath the tree were filled with thoughtful gifts, some with name tags. Others to be used in games that were planned. The DJ had arrived just before Roz left the restaurant to shower and change, and minutes after Pierre entered the side door looking delicious and devilish dressed in black. She knew he was there to finish what Riviera and the other cooks had started, to make sure every dish was perfect for his baby girl. They talked for less than five minutes before she headed out, but he'd called her after leaving the Ritz. Roz knew that Lisette's dream would come true.

When Roz entered the room, its final transformation almost took her breath away. She pulled out her phone and snapped pictures of the sparkly wonderland. Hearing laughter, she looked up and saw Stefanie flirting with the DJ. "Figures," Roz mumbled, walking over with a smile.

The two friends went outside and were talking to Buddha when Lisette and her entourage arrived. They stood in silence as the uniformed driver opened the door with a flourish and seven stylishly dressed ladies exited the car. As beautiful as they all were, Lisette was a diamond in the cluster of jewels. Her long black hair was swept up in a loose chignon with a few wispy curls tumbling over her shoulder. Roz's gift to her, a deep red velvet stretch mini with long sleeves and peekaboo shoulders, emphasized the hourglass shape that regular workouts and good genes had designed. Roz watched her carefully walk toward the steps on beaded heels.

Buddha raced down to help her ascend. She stopped and gave Roz a big hug.

"This is so beautiful!"

Roz laughed, hugging her tightly. "You haven't even seen the room!"

"I don't have to. Pierre told me it was amazing, just like you."

"He said that?"

"I added that last part."

Roz walked inside with Lisette, wanting to see her face at the big reveal. They reached the closed door. Lisette started to open it, then turned once again.

"I talked to Mom earlier today. She told me about calling you, asking for your help in changing Pierre's mind. I know you tried. Thanks for that."

"You're welcome, Liz. Don't give up on your brother. Healing takes time."

"I know." Lisette took a deep breath, opened the door and screamed. The DJ fired up the music. Cocktail hour had begun.

Roz sneaked away and found Pierre in the kitchen.

"They'll be here at eight," he whispered. His eyes almost sparkled as he gave Roz a quick kiss, then stirred the gumbo appetizer a final time. He reached for a spoon, dipped it in the pot and lifted it to Roz's lips. She blew on it gently before tasting it.

"That's almost better than sex," she whispered back.

"You think so, huh? Later on, trust me, I'll make sure that's not the case."

At seven forty-five, thirty invited guests found their names on ornamental place cards and sat down. Roz walked over to Lisette and led her to the center table, where they both seated themselves. Roz purposely placed Lisette with her back to the door.

"Who's sitting in those seats?" she asked.

"Pierre will sit here," Roz said, pointing to the chair beside her. "Then three lucky winners will get to join the princess center stage."

"Then we've got to rig the game, because my two besties need to be here and we have to make sure Craig is sitting next to me."

"I thought I felt some rhythm between you two. He's cute."

Lisette winked and beamed.

Just before eight the door opened and a line of waiters entered carrying the first course. Pierre entered behind

them. He'd changed from his chef's whites and wore a
black Armani suit with a black silk shirt and striped tie.

"When are we going to start the game?" Lisette whispered. "I want my friends to join me."

Roz looked beyond the birthday girl's shoulder. "I think
we'll fill those seats right now. We have some late arrivals."

With a slight frown, Lisette turned around, just as Lana
entered, followed by Chloe and Bernard. Lisette's mouth
dropped as she stared wide-eyed at Roz and Pierre, then
over at the rest of her family. She ran to hug them, her joy
so effusive it lit every corner of the room.

Several hours later, a partied-out Roz and exhausted
Pierre entered his home and headed straight for the bedroom.

"I think I'm going to take a bath, babe. I don't have the
strength to stand up for a shower."

"Should I join you?"

"I was hoping you would."

Pierre filled the tub, turned on the jets and then eased
into the swirling water. He reached for Roz as she entered
and pulled her against him. She shifted to lean her head
on his shoulder.

"Tonight was amazing, babe. Lisette was so happy,"
she murmured.

"I know. When we took the family picture I don't know
which was brighter, the flash or her smile."

"What did you think about Dr. Stern?"

"I didn't want to like the man who took away my mama.
But she told me how he reacted when she finally came
clean and told him about us."

Roz looked at him. "What did he do?"

"She said he cried. Can you believe that? A stranger
crying for us? She said it hurt him to know that she'd car-

ried that burden alone all these years, and that they could have raised more children together."

"Wow."

"That's what I said. Mom wants us to plan a vacation, go somewhere all together where we can talk, and get to know each other."

"Sounds like a wonderful idea."

"Will you come with me?"

"I'm not family."

"Yes, but you're the reason I have one again."

They kissed.

"Hey, how's the job search going?" he eventually asked.

"Slow."

"Are you okay financially? Because if not, don't be proud. Let me know. It's because of me you're not working."

"I appreciate that, but right now I'm okay. As long as I can pay my mortgage, I can survive."

"You could always move in here. I'm hardly home and there's plenty of room."

"What, so you can throw me out the first time we have a fight? No, thank you. I only stay in homes where my name is on the paperwork."

"Hmm."

The two finished their bath and climbed into bed, ready to make love. Their minds said yes. Their bodies said no. Pierre asked for a morning rain check, and they spooned their bodies together beneath the covers. Roz went to sleep with a smile on her face, totally unaware that she'd given Pierre an idea for the perfect way to show his eternal gratitude.

Chapter 31

Roz stepped out of the shower into one of three rooms that made up the master bath. Pierre's offer for her to move in was more than generous, and had surprised her. The house was beyond amazing, more beautiful than any she'd ever seen or imagined. But Roz had worked hard to become a home owner and felt more comfortable in her nineteenth century bungalow than she'd ever felt growing up in East-over. Those emotional scabs from her formative years had healed, but the scar remained. She wondered if she could ever be comfortable in a house that could fit her bunga-low in it ten times over.

After brushing her curls into a ponytail, Roz shimmied into her underwear and headed to the walk-in closet for the colorful maxi she'd recently ordered online. Just as she stepped into black, flat sandals, Pierre walked in and wrapped his arms around her.

She gasped. "Pierre! You just scared the bejeebers out of me!"

"Sorry about that," he said with a laugh.

"Sure. Sorry, not sorry. What are you doing here?"

"I live here, remember?"

"You know what I mean. It's seven o'clock on a Satur-day, the restaurant's busiest night. Did you forget some-thing? You could have called and I would have brought it to you."

"I didn't forget anything, but I did come to pick some-thing up."

"What?"

"You."

"Me?"

"Yes, and it looks like you're dressed up to go somewhere, so my timing is perfect."

"Really? You'll come with me to an art exhibit? You might like it," Roz continued, reaching for a pair of silver hoops and a bracelet to complete her outfit. "It's over at the—"

"Doesn't matter where it is," Pierre interrupted, grabbing her hand. "We'll have to do that another time."

"Pierre, wait. You can't just change my plans like that and expect me to go with you."

"Why not?"

"How do you figure that what you have in mind is better or more important than the plans I've made?"

"Because I made the plans, that's how I know."

Roz stopped, pulled her hand out of his grip. "I'm serious, Pierre. I've been looking forward to seeing this exhibit ever since I heard it was coming to town. Not only that, but this is work related. I'll be taking notes for a story that will hopefully sell."

Pierre leaned against the wall, crossing his arms as he pondered her statement. "Look, I took the night off to spend it with you. You were right with what you said the other night. We've never had a proper date. Except for Mondays, I'm always working. And I'm not even off then. You deserve more than Monday night, early mornings and French Quarter kisses in the middle of the night."

"Listen to you, sounding all poetic. French Quarter kisses, huh? Did you come up with that all by yourself?"

"Was that special?"

"Quite. I appreciate you wanting to take me out. I just wish you'd called to let me know."

"Tell you what. We'll do both. Make a quick stop where I wanted to take you and then, if you still insist on going, stop by wherever it is you want to go."

"If according to you we're doing both, I won't have to insist, will I?"

He kissed her on the nose. "You're so smart. Now come on. I don't want to be late."

Roz was peeved, but she bit back a sarcastic response, grabbed her purse and walked with Pierre to the garage. She headed toward the SUV, but he passed it and continued on to his "baby," the black Ferrari.

"We're riding in this?"

Pierre smiled, opened her door, then jogged to the other side of the car and got in.

"Where are we going?"

"You'll see soon enough."

"Must be someplace special since we're riding in style. Am I dressed okay?"

"You look beautiful and don't go there with your story, okay? Just accept the compliment."

"You're right. I will. Thank you."

For the next thirty minutes, the two listened to music and shared small talk. Roz relaxed and decided to enjoy the evening. She even began to get excited about going out. That it was a Saturday night did make it special. She knew how much of a control freak Pierre could be in the kitchen, so for him to trust his sous chef on this busy night showed both his confidence in Riviera and his thoughtfulness toward her.

Relaxing worked for a while. But the farther they traveled, the more confused she became. Until he exited the freeway.

"We're going to Ma's?"

Pierre reached out and grabbed her hand. "Can't put anything past you, huh?"

"You know I love Ma's cooking, but really, Pierre? We skipped the exhibit for a bowl of jambalaya? The exhibit is on tour and only here for a weekend. We could eat at Ma's anytime."

He said nothing, which rankled Roz even more.

"Do you even know if she's open? If there are no customers, Ma will close up."

"We'll see."

She pouted in silence, taking in the drab surroundings of the Ninth Ward. Amid the deterioration and neglect, the Ferrari stood out like a beacon. Parking it in front of Ma's humble abode made the contrast even starker.

"I don't know if driving this car here was a good idea."

"We'll be fine."

Pierre got out of the vehicle and came around to her door. Roz leaned forward, her eyes narrowed as she checked out the house.

"Did Ma paint her place?"

"Looks like maybe she did."

"It's nice. Looks like that might be a new screen door, too. Wait, is that a doorbell? Wow, Ma is going uptown!"

Pierre opened the door and then moved back to let Roz enter. One step, and her jaw dropped. "Oh my God! Ma!"

Ma came from the kitchen wearing a smile as white as her apron. "Who's that making so much noise?"

"Ma, your place! What…what happened?"

"Your man there happened, that's what."

Roz's head whipped around. "You?" He nodded. "You!" She gave him a playful swat, then looked around a room totally different than what had been here before. Drab walls were now painted a bright yellow. Laminate flooring with a slate blue, pale yellow, gray and black geometric design replaced worn, gray carpeting. Plastic tables and chairs had been replaced by ones made of ebony wood. They were topped with black-and-white-checkered tablecloths, and mason jar centerpieces filled with glass beads and fabric flowers. Roz's heart swelled as she took it all in.

"Ah! The pictures!"

Black-and-white photos in black frames decorated the walls. Pictures of Ma's dishes, one of her hand holding a wooden spoon stirring a steamy concoction, one her signature red pail of crawfish and one of a newspaper-covered table littered with shells. It was all so unexpected Roz felt herself tear up.

Pierre put an arm around her. "What do you think?"

"I'm speechless." She looked at Pierre, thought about how nasty she'd been on the way over. "Babe…"

"Don't worry about it. You didn't know."

"This is amazing, Ma."

Ma's eyes sparkled with pride. "This is the best part." She crooked her finger for Roz to follow. They walked into the kitchen, where once again Roz was shocked. The small room had been totally updated and reconfigured to maximize the space. Top-of-the-line stainless appliances, large wooden cutting boards on quartz countertops. Sparkling copper and stainless pots and pans hung from a stainless and copper rack, ready to join the covered ones on the stove emitting aromas that made Roz's mouth water.

"Babe, this was so nice of you to do for Ma."

He shrugged. "It wasn't much."

"It's everything," Ma corrected. "All I ever wanted," she told Roz. "Which is why I told him that the only way I'd accept all of this kindness was if he made sure that he was my very first customer to eat in this new space. So I'm going to shoo you out of my kitchen. Go wash your hands!"

Pierre and Roz settled at a corner table that offered a

view of the entire room. She reached for his hands and clasped them. "You're pretty amazing, you know that?"

He popped an imaginary collar. "So I've been told."

They both laughed.

"When did all this happen??"

"Last week. Working in Ma's kitchen showed me just how limiting that configuration was. That's where the idea started. As she and I talked, and later, when I had my manager locate a designer, I realized that it wouldn't cost that much more to redo the living/dining area, too. Ma was so appreciative, but not as much as I am for what she shared with me, her recipes and our shared history. That conversation is what brought me around to seeing my mom, began to thaw the ice around my heart. To bring someone that kind of happiness, I'd do it all over again."

Ma came out swinging her signature crawfish in one hand, a roll of newspaper under the other arm. Soon Pierre and Roz were twisting, sucking and chucking, wiping juice off their fingers and mouths. Steaming dishes of red beans and rice, jambalaya and Ma's special sausage over steamed vegetables and rice were presented, washed down with ice-cold lemon water.

Pierre ate most of the sausage dish, then put down his fork. "Okay, there is another reason I brought you here."

"What?"

"Two, actually. I want you to go on the vacation with my family, and I want you to move in with me."

Roz shook her head. "The first family vacation should just be family, and as long as I can have unlimited visits to your place, I'm totally fine in my bungalow."

"But look at all the money you'll save."

"Gotta make money to save money."

"You're making my point. Why do some women have

to be so independent that they refuse the offer when a man is trying to help them?"

"You want to help me? Pay off my mortgage. The one to the house with the deed that has my name on it."

"Okay."

"Pierre, I'm kidding, and not trying to be difficult. I'm happy with you and life just the way it is. I've only been out of a job a short while. Once the holidays are over and people get back to business I'll hit the streets in earnest and probably be back to work before January is over. In the meantime, I'm doing a little freelance. A little editing. I'll be okay."

Ma came out of the kitchen, wiping her hands on an apron. "Y'all want something else to drink?"

Roz shook her head. "Water's fine for me."

"What about you, Pierre?"

"This is our first Saturday night date," he said, with a wink at Roz. "Why don't we mark the occasion with something bubbly?"

"That's sweet, babe, but I really don't want a soda."

"Me either. I was thinking something grander, like champagne."

"Yeah, right. You redid her place but I don't think Ma redid her menu."

Ma looked from Pierre to Roz and back. "Let me see what I can find."

"If you have something sweet, Ma, that would be great, too."

"I don't see how you can eat another bite," Roz said. "I'm stuffed."

"Just a bite is all I want."

Ma was gone only a moment. She returned with two helpings of praline cream, two crystal flutes and a bottle of premium champagne. "I don't know much about the different brands. Will this one do?"

Roz's eyes widened. She looked at Pierre, took in the smirk on his face. "What are you up to?"

"What do you mean?"

"Don't sit over there acting innocent. One doesn't simply stumble across a three-hundred-dollar bottle of champagne. You bought it, right?"

"Maybe."

"Well, why not just say so? Why are you acting all… weird?" Roz picked up her spoon and dug into the dessert. "Have you had this, Pierre? It is my absolute favorite!"

"You're really going to like that bowl," Ma said as she walked away. "I outdid myself this time."

Pierre opened the champagne, watching Roz devour the pie.

"What happened to you wanting only one bite?"

"Can't do it with this," Roz mumbled around a mouthful. She happily dug in for another spoonful, then froze.

Pierre finished filling the glasses. "What's the matter?"

Roz leaned forward, with furtive glances toward the kitchen. "Don't say anything, but I think there's something in my dessert."

"Something in your dessert?" Pierre said loudly.

"Pierre, I—" Roz's teeth remained gritted as Ma hurried to the table.

"Who said something was in their food?" Ma's indignant look was accompanied by a hand on her hip. "I run a clean establishment here and take pride in my work. You're not going to find anything in my food."

"I'm sorry, Ma. It's just that…" Roz gingerly placed the spoon into the creamy, crumbling ensemble. She looked up apologetically. "There's something in here, Ma."

"Well, what is it?"

Roz scraped with her spoon until hitting what felt like the hard shell of a long-dead bug or crustacean. She placed her spoon beneath it, her stomach roiling as, with one eye closed and the other barely opened, she lifted the foreign object out of the bowl and quickly made an observation.

Bugs didn't sparkle. She screamed anyway. "Oh my God!"

"There you go, child. A five-carat roach in your food."

Pierre burst out laughing as Ma sauntered back to the kitchen, her culinary reputation intact.

"Pierre, what is this?"

"A way to get you to go on vacation and move into my house."

Roz gave him a look.

He smiled, pulled the ring from the spoon and wiped it off. "It's the only way I could think of to convey how much you mean to me. The only way I could insure that the woman who came into my life, turned it upside down and then all the way around, never left it."

He stood, walked to her side of the table and placed one knee on the newly tiled floor. "So will you do it?"

"Do what?" Roz whispered.

Pierre huffed. "Move in, woman, and go on vacation!"

"Pierre!" Roz laughed, and smacked his shoulder.

"Quit playing in there and ask her nicely," Ma commanded from the kitchen, yelling at Pierre just like a mother would.

It couldn't have been more perfect for Roz, and neither could his next four words.

"Will you marry me?"

She tilted her head as if to ponder the question. "I don't know. A byline reading Rosalyn LeBlanc..."

"Y'all are going to kill me in here," Ma lamented, blatantly eavesdropping and unashamed.

"Yes, babe. I'll marry you."

The promise was sealed with a kiss.

"Come on out here, Ma," Roz shouted, "and bring another glass. Since you were a crucial part of the proposal, you might as well be a part of the toast."

Pierre's proposal was a memorable ending to a monumental year and the precursor to a new one filled with realignments, repercussions and revelations.

Roz's engagement announcement sent those closest to her over the moon. Stefanie had all but taken over the New Year wedding plans, delaying her own nuptials to do so. Lisette appointed herself as Stefanie's assistant, only right she'd stated when asked, for the incredible party Roz organized for her.

Roz didn't mind. In fact she was grateful. Her hands were full working as an editor-at-large for a national magazine, a job that was landed following the article she'd written and submitted on the traveling art show she saw the day after Pierre's engagement.

After a random encounter at Café du Monde, Roz and Ginny reconnected. Through her Roz learned that the once-thriving paper she worked for was beginning to struggle. Papers stayed afloat largely through advertising and several major accounts had pulled their business. Roz would never wish anyone harm but couldn't help thinking the downturn was Andy getting a dose of the karma he put out coming back to bite him. She also learned that he and Paige were indeed an item and had taken the relationship public. Their dating was of no surprise to Roz. She felt each was exactly what the other deserved.

It was late February when Roz pulled Pierre's Christmas gift into one of his garage's six parking spaces. She'd felt the sleek, silver BMW a gift far more extravagant than she deserved or needed, but he had insisted, the same way he'd bugged her until she gave in and agreed to move into his home. A cute, young couple now enjoyed the bungalow she now owned and rented out.

Roz exited the car and dashed toward the door as drops of rain began to fall. Once inside she entered the kitchen and noticed a beautifully wrapped gift box on the counter. Her intrigue with what it was doing there only increased as she looked at the tag and saw her name. She gently unwrapped the paper and removed the box's lid. Inside was another box, a telltale Tiffany blue. She opened it and found a beautiful silver bracelet with a single, heart-shaped charm. She lifted it out of the box and noticed a message had been engraved.

I won.

"Won what?" Roz mumbled, as she undid the clasp and slipped the bracelet on her arm. Later, when Pierre came home, she found out the meaning. Which led to kisses in the Quarter, and so much more, all night long.

* * * * *

COMING NEXT MONTH
Available July 17, 2018

#581 ONE PERFECT MOMENT
The Taylors of Temptation • **by A.C. Arthur**
TV producer Ava Cannon is stunned to discover that the lover who briefly shared her bed is one of America's most famous sextuplets. But Dr. Gage Taylor now shuns the spotlight. As they rekindle their affair, will Ava have to choose between a game-changing career move and her love?

#582 CAMPAIGN FOR HIS HEART
The Cardinal House • **by Joy Avery**
Former foster child Lauder Tolson is running for North Carolina state senate, but he needs a girlfriend for the campaign. The ideal candidate is childhood nemesis Willow Dawson. To fulfill her own dream, she agrees. Soon, they're a devoted couple in public, but neither expects how hot it gets in private.

#583 PATH TO PASSION
The Astacios • **by Nana Prah**
Heir to his family's global empire, branding genius Miguel Astacio turns everything into marketing gold. Only his best friend's sister seems immune to his magic touch. Until Tanya Carrington comes to him to save her floundering nightclub. Miguel is ready to rectify past mistakes. But will he win her heart?

#584 UNCONDITIONALLY MINE
Miami Dreams • **by Nadine Gonzalez**
Event planner Sofia Silva is keeping a secret. No one can know that her engagement to her cheating fiancé is over. Until she meets gorgeous, wealthy newcomer Jonathan Gunther. When he invites Sofia to lie low at his house, their attraction explodes…but will her dilemma ruin their chance at forever?

Get 2 Free Books,
Plus 2 Free Gifts—
just for trying the
Reader Service!

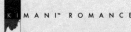

At three minutes after six, Gage was standing at the door
of the deck once more, smiling up at Ava as she stepped
slowly onto the yacht.

"You look beautiful," he said, taking her hand to help
her on board. "I'm so glad you're here."

And he was, Gage thought as he looked down into her
deep brown eyes. He was glad to see her in the short blue
dress that might have seemed plain on anyone else but
her. She wore a blue-and-beige scarf draped around her
neck and black boots to her calf. Her hair was free and
flowing so that she had a fresh and innocently enticing
look. Yes, he was glad she was here.

"I almost didn't come," she said and then shook her head as if trying to dismiss the words. "I meant to say thank you. I'm looking forward to a great evening."

He heard the words and saw the small smile she offered, but Gage wasn't buying it. Her eyes and the slight slump in her shoulders said differently.

"Is something wrong, Ava? Did something happen to you today?"

"No," she said and waved her hand over her face like she needed to wipe away whatever was bothering her. "I'm fine. It's nothing. Let's just have dinner."

"Sure. Everything's ready," Gage told her.

He led her to the table and pulled out the matching bronzed iron chair, all the while thinking that she was a horrible liar. Something was definitely wrong with her, and he was determined to find out what.

So he could fix it. Gage knew in that instant that he would do anything to take that look off her face. Anything at all.

Don't miss One Perfect Moment
by A.C. Arthur, available August 2018
wherever Harlequin® Kimani Romance™
books and ebooks are sold.

Want to give in to temptation with
steamy tales of irresistible desire?

Check out **Harlequin® Presents®,
Harlequin® Desire** and
Harlequin® Kimani™ Romance books!

New books available every month!

CONNECT WITH US AT:

Harlequin.com/Community

 Facebook.com/HarlequinBooks

 Twitter.com/HarlequinBooks

 Instagram.com/HarlequinBooks

 Pinterest.com/HarlequinBooks

ReaderService.com

**ROMANCE WHEN
YOU NEED IT**

PGENRE2017